SHE WASN'T SUPPOSED
TO FEEL LIKE THIS....

Susanna stood just inside the house, leaning back against the door. Adrenaline flooded her veins and her heart thumped as if she'd just narrowly escaped some grave danger. And in a way, maybe she had. She and Anders had almost ended their fake date with a not-so-fake goodnight kiss.

Susanna hugged herself, her whole body trembling. Why had she let her guard down? When Anders touched her shoulder, she knew it was time to get away, to put some distance between them. Instead, his hand on her skin was like a match striking. She'd been flooded with a sudden blazing warmth, and when he moved toward her, she'd responded instinctively. They'd come so close. . . .

Her heart was still slamming against her rib cage, and she couldn't prevent her slightly dizzy thoughts from taking her to a forbidden place. What if she *hadn't* drawn away? What if his hand had slid from her shoulder to the back of her neck? What if his lips had brushed hers . . . ?

S0-AZQ-998

Don't miss any of the books in *Love Stories*
—the romantic series from Bantam Books!

Love Stories

it's a
prom
thing

Diane Schwemm

BANTAM BOOKS
NEW YORK · TORONTO · LONDON · SYDNEY · AUCKLAND

To Johanna and Fridtjos

RL 6, age 12 and up

IT'S A PROM THING

A Bantam Book / June 1997

Produced by Daniel Weiss Associates, Inc.
33 West 17th Street
New York, NY 10011.
Cover photography by Michael Segal.

ISBN: 0-553-57075-7

Published simultaneously in the United States and Canada

Bantam Books are published by Bantam Books, a division of Bantam
Doubleday Dell Publishing Group, Inc. Its trademark, consisting of the
words "Bantam Books" and the portrayal of a rooster, is Registered in
U.S. Patent and Trademark Office and in other countries. Marca
Registrada. Bantam Books, 1540 Broadway, New York, New York 10036.

PRINTED IN THE UNITED STATES OF AMERICA

OPM   0 9 8 7 6 5 4 3 2

ONE

"WOULDN'T YOU KNOW the school wouldn't get around to doing something this cool until the second semester of our senior year?" Carly Donovan said as she took an appreciative sip of her steaming-hot double latte.

The Altavista High cafeteria had just installed a coffee bar, and on this rainy January day, the line for espressos and cappuccinos was practically out the door. Susanna Reyes spooned into the whipped cream on top of her large mocha. "Better late than never," she replied.

Carly lingered on the senior-year theme. "It's our last semester at A.H.S.," she said, tilting her head so that her wavy, bright blond hair spilled over one shoulder. "Only five more months and we're out of here. Isn't that weird?"

Susanna smiled, her brown eyes twinkling. "What's weird is that we've eaten lunch in this

1

room every single day for three and a half years and we *always* sit at the same table."

Jin-Seung Lee laughed. "We're not the only ones. The cheerleaders always sit at that table." She pointed toward the cafeteria entrance.

"For maximum visibility," Kate Greenberg suggested.

"And the smokers always sit there," Jin went on.

"So they can get out into the courtyard and light up fast," Carly contributed.

"And the jocks always sit right by the lunch line," Jin finished.

"So they can continuously carbo-load with the least expenditure of energy," said Susanna.

"So what have we established here?" wondered Kate, her gray eyes crinkling with amusement.

"The more things change, the more they stay the same?" guessed Carly.

"Something like that," Jin agreed.

Susanna cupped her coffee in both hands, gazing thoughtfully toward the window. Outside, rain dripped steadily from the branches of the massive redwood trees that flanked the school building. *The more things change, the more they stay the same,* she mused. Personally, she wasn't so sure about that. In her own experience recently, the more things changed, the more things changed, and sometimes they changed for the worse. And change was forever.

Kate and Jin had risen to their feet and were gathering up their books. "Concert choir meeting," Jin explained. "See you guys in bio?"

2

The four girls took advanced placement biology together during sixth period. "You bet," Carly confirmed.

When she and Susanna were alone, Carly pushed her coffee cup aside and leaned forward with her elbows on the table. "Earth to Susanna. Can you read me?"

Susanna blinked. "Sorry. Did I miss something?"

"Not really." Carly studied her best friend's face. "I just worry about you when you disappear like that."

Susanna sat up straighter and flashed a big smile. "Is that better?"

Carly nodded approvingly. "One hundred percent. You look so great these days, Suze! I wish *I'd* gotten to go to Hawaii for Christmas vacation."

"Nothing like a suntan," Susanna admitted.

"It's not just the tan," Carly noted. "You seem a lot more . . . I don't know. More like your old self."

Susanna hunched her shoulders slightly, folding her arms across her chest. "Maybe," she said, her tone guarded.

Carly's bright blue eyes were warm with sympathy. "I know it's been terrible for you, Suze. But at some point, you have to put the past behind you and make a fresh start. You're the prettiest, smartest girl at A.H.S. You've got the world at your fingertips. And after all, it's—"

"Second semester of our senior year." Susanna had to laugh. "I know, I know."

"So, I sound like a broken record," Carly remarked ruefully. "I have your best interests at heart, Suze."

"I know you do," Susanna said quietly. "It's just that—"

She stopped midsentence to look up at the handsome, broad-shouldered boy in faded jeans and a baggy flannel shirt who'd materialized next to their table. Jason Rivers, co-captain of the Altavista High football team, spun an empty chair around and straddled it backward. "Don't know about you two, but I've got a nice little caffeine buzz going." He grinned at Susanna. "Teachers must've come up with this coffee bar idea. Finally, something guaranteed to keep us all awake during class."

Susanna smiled. "Bet you still doze off in English."

"Knock me upside the head with your Cliffs Notes if I do," he said. He paused for a moment. "So. Just wanted to let you know I'm having a party Friday night."

"Great," said Carly.

Jason's eyes were on Susanna. She felt him nudge her foot gently under the table. "Think you can make it, Suze? We never got to go out and celebrate after acing Paulson's calculus final last month. You were going to let me buy you dinner, remember?"

Susanna nodded, but she couldn't speak. There was a tight feeling in her chest just as there'd been a few minutes earlier when Carly had started talking about making a fresh start.

"My parents'll be out of town," Jason pressed. "It'll rock."

"Um," Susanna mumbled, "Thanks, Jason, but I might be—" Just as she was about to say "busy," Carly kicked her hard in the shin. "Uh, sure," Susanna said, trying not to wince. "I'll be there."

4

"Great." As he stood up, Jason rested a hand briefly on Susanna's shoulder. "See you."

When Jason had sauntered off, Carly wiggled her eyebrows at Susanna. "Jason Rivers. *Whoa.*"

"We're in A.P. math together," Susanna said.

"Solving the equation of love?" Carly quipped.

"He invited you too," Susanna pointed out.

"Yeah, but he didn't gaze deeply into my eyes while doing so. And did I detect a little footsie?"

"I'm not looking for a boyfriend, Carly," Susanna stated in no uncertain terms.

"I didn't say you were. This is going to be fun, Suze!" Carly's eyes sparkled. "You and me, hitting the party scene, just like old times."

Susanna wished she could share Carly's enthusiasm. If she thought really hard, she could remember the "old times" Carly was referring to, but it was kind of like watching a movie of someone else's life. They were definitely a little wild and crazy, Susanna recalled, an eye-catching, attention-getting foursome. Blond bombshell Carly; Kate, the outspoken redhead; delicately beautiful Jin-Seung; and Susanna, the creative, adventurous one with the "natural" good looks. *Did we have fun?* Susanna wrinkled her forehead. Yeah, sure, it was a blast partying at the beach and going to concerts and all that other stuff, and although Susanna had never been as boy crazy as Carly, she'd had plenty of dates. But all that was before she got serious with Seth. *"Just like old times"—no way,* thought Susanna with a tiny sigh. *There's before, and there's after. Nothing's the same as it was. Nothing.*

Carly shifted gears in rapid-fire fashion, as she often did. "So, tell me that new Norwegian exchange student isn't the most spectacularly beautiful specimen of manhood you've ever laid eyes on," she said in a low, reverent tone.

"What Norwegian exchange student?"

"Two tables over. Check him out," Carly instructed.

Susanna turned her head dutifully. She saw a tall boy with a rangy build and wavy brown hair trying to eat his lunch. He didn't have much elbowroom, though. He was surrounded by girls—the entire A.H.S. varsity cheerleading squad was playing Welcome Wagon. "Didn't take long for the vultures to descend," Susanna observed.

"Can you blame them?" asked Carly. "I plan to take a more subtle approach, but I'm dying to get my hands on him. Look at that body. That face!"

Susanna tossed a paper napkin at her friend. "Drool alert."

"Come on, admit it—he's gorgeous," said Carly. "In fact, he looks a lot like that Sven guy you had the hots for a few summers ago."

"His name was Thor," said Susanna.

"Whatever. Your type anyhow. But don't get any ideas."

"You won't have any competition from me," Susanna assured her.

"That's right. *You'll* be busy with Jason Rivers."

Susanna didn't waste her breath denying it. Carly wasn't listening anyway—she was busy scheming up ways to get to know the exchange student. Susanna let her friend ramble, it gave her time to think. *She's wrong about my "type" of guy, but she's right about some things,* Susanna mused. This *was* their last semester of high school, and she'd miss out on a lot if she kept hiding at home. When she thought about going to Jason's party, though, her palms started to sweat. It was sort of, kind of, almost, too much like a date.

I'm still not ready, Susanna thought. When other guys had called her in recent weeks, she'd politely told them all no. She'd just have to come up with an excuse to cancel on Jason.

Anders Lund shifted uncomfortably in his seat, silently wishing that Americans, especially female Americans, weren't quite so friendly. He'd only just met these girls, and already they were touching his arm when they spoke to him, pulling their chairs so close that their knees bumped against his, and offering to buy him things.

"Let me get you another sandwich," offered Rachel Berman, bestowing a ravishing smile on him as she hopped to her feet.

"No, I bet you're in the mood for ice cream," guessed Chelsea Ladislaw, her voice a seductive purr. "How about Rocky Road?"

Anders didn't know what she was talking about. Was that a flavor? "Er . . ."

"Or how about a cup of coffee?" cut in Alicia Van Etten, fluttering her long eyelashes. "We have mocha, latte, double latte, cappuccino, espresso . . ."

7

She continued to reel off the choices. Growing more and more confused, Anders felt his tentative grasp of English slipping. Was she even speaking English? "Please to slow down," he begged with a rueful smile. "I can listen only to some of the words. I need to get . . . how do you say? More vocabulary."

The girls all laughed delightedly, as if he'd said the most amusing thing in the world. "I just *love* your accent," declared Tiffany Stone. She turned to Shannon O'Malley. "Isn't his accent great? Don't you love it?"

"It's great. I love it," Shannon confirmed.

Anders wasn't sure how to reply, or whether to reply at all. What would he say—"Thanks, I love your accent too"? He cast a somewhat desperate glance around the cafeteria, wishing one of the guys he'd met that morning in homeroom—Antonio, Jason, or Rick—would rescue him. *How did I end up at a table full of girls anyhow?* he wondered.

Just then, Rachel returned to the table carrying another one of those huge, American-style sandwiches that had, in Anders's opinion, way too many different items piled between slices of basically tasteless bread. At the same moment, Chelsea arrived with an enormous bowl of ice cream. Last but not least, Alicia offered up what looked like a Styrofoam cup full of whipped cream, though Anders guessed there was some fancy coffee lurking underneath.

"Thank you. It is very nice of you," said Anders, giving each girl a shy smile and mustering up his appetite as best he could.

At least digging into the sandwich gave him an

excuse not to talk for a few minutes. He didn't really enjoy being the center of attention. By nature, he was quiet and reserved . . . not that the girls had noticed.

Is it the U.S. or just California? Anders asked himself as he polished off the sandwich and moved on to the ice cream. Everything and everyone seemed to move so fast. People talked fast and drove fast—even in a small, peaceful town like Altavista, tucked in the redwoods of Marin County, north of San Francisco.

For the first time since his plane had landed two days earlier, Anders found himself wondering if he'd done the right thing by coming to the United States during the latter half of his final year of secondary school. *It would have been easier to stay in Bergen,* he thought. He shot a sideways glance at Tiffany, Rachel, Shannon, Chelsea, and Alicia. They looked like hungry tigresses, waiting to pounce. *Safer too!*

Anders reminded himself that he'd picked Altavista High because it had an excellent language program and he hoped to earn a degree in international relations someday. And maybe the girls were kind of overwhelming, but they were just trying to be nice. He could deal with it.

"You know, if you want help with your English, I'd be an *excellent* tutor," Chelsea offered.

Alicia arched her pale blond eyebrows at Chelsea. "As I recall, you *bombed* the American lit final last semester. Anders doesn't want to learn English from an illiterate." She placed a hand on Anders's arm. "Let *me* tutor you."

"*I'm* in A.P. English," Rachel cut in, gripping

Anders's other arm. "You'll learn tons more from *me*."

Shannon hurried to present her own credentials. "Well, *I* write for the school newspaper. I could help you with your writing assignments better than anyone!"

Anders looked from one girl to another, taken aback by the intensity of this impromptu competition. "Thank you, that is much generosity, but I am not needing a tutor," he said quickly. "I do better working on my own."

"If you change your mind . . ." Chelsea scribbled something on a scrap of paper and pressed it into his palm.

Not to be outdone, the other girls started scribbling too. A few seconds later, Anders had a handful of telephone numbers. When the bell rang, he jumped to his feet in relief.

He wasn't free yet. "I'll walk you to class," Tiffany offered, "since you probably still don't know your way around too well."

"So will I," said Rachel.

"Me too," Alicia chimed in.

Anders tolerated being escorted out of the cafeteria by all five girls. *If my friends back in Bergen could see me now!* he thought wryly, hoping his face wasn't turning too red. The girls were all knockouts—he felt as if he were on a Hollywood movie set. Yes, any other guy in his situation would be eating up the attention. But other guys hadn't known Jennifer. . . .

Anders didn't realize that being in the United States, in Jennifer's home state of California, would bring back

10

all the old memories with such intensity. But as he looked at Tiffany and Rachel and the others, he could only see one perfect face, one pair of emerald green eyes. *Jennifer,* Anders thought with pained longing.

Susanna flashed her volunteer's badge at the attendant as she steered her secondhand Honda Civic into the county hospital parking lot after school. She considered dropping in on her mother, a doctor who spent two days a week at the hospital's free clinic for migrant farmworkers, but her watch told her she was running late. Grabbing a large leather art portfolio from the backseat, she hurried to the elevator bank and pressed the button for the third floor.

Inside the hospital, she strode briskly down the corridor toward Ward F. As she got closer, she started recognizing the staff. "Hello, Sherry," she called to a middle-aged nurse in crisp white trousers and a pink smock. She waved to another, younger nurse. "Hi, Karen."

"Susanna!" Sherry grinned. "Good to see you."

"Happy New Year," Karen said.

"Same to you," Susanna replied cheerfully. She paused at the registration desk to smile at a handsome but tired-looking intern in baggy, toothpaste-green scrubs. "Looked in a mirror lately, Bob?" she teased.

Bob raked a hand through his rumpled sandy hair. "Cut me some slack, Reyes. My chief's on vacation, so I'm stuck with extra call. I haven't slept in about a week."

Susanna pretended to play the violin. "Poor Bob," she said in a tragic tone.

11

He smiled wryly. "And Santa didn't bring me the shiny red wagon I wanted for Christmas either."

She laughed. "I'll buy you a soda later, how about that?"

The patients' lounge was already packed when Susanna got there. There were both new and familiar faces, and the kids ranged in age from about five to thirteen years old. Some wore bathrobes over hospital gowns while others were dressed in pajamas or sweat suits. Some seemed to have a lot of energy while others appeared weaker. They were almost all losing their hair from chemotherapy. Baseball caps and colorful bandannas were very popular.

Susanna felt her throat tighten as she gazed into their eager, expectant eyes, but she bit back the tears. She didn't come here to cry over these children, although sometimes when she got into the car after her weekly visit, she'd rest her head on the steering wheel and burst into tears.

"So, who's ready for some art?" she asked, opening her portfolio on top of the table.

Hands shot into the air. "Me, me, me!" the kids chorused.

"We're going to try collage today," Susanna informed them, laying out the supplies she'd brought. "I've got a little of everything here: construction paper, old magazines to cut up, different colors of yarn, feathers, glitter, seeds, sequins, Magic Markers, finger paint."

"But how do we do it, Suze?" asked one little girl, her earnest brown eyes large in a thin, pale face.

Susanna couldn't resist giving Becky a quick

hug. Did the child seem more fragile than the last time Susanna had seen her? "That's the great thing about collage," Susanna answered. "You can do whatever you want. You can make a picture or tell a story or just experiment with color and pattern and texture. There are absolutely no rules."

"Just don't eat the glue," quipped ten-year-old Marcus.

"Right." Susanna cocked her index finger at him, grinning. "No glue eating or we get in big trouble with Dr. Benitez."

The kids set to work on their collages with enthusiasm. A low hum of happy chatter filled the room. Susanna circulated, giving tips and admiring the works in progress. When Dr. Benitez stuck her head in the room, Susanna went to the door to speak with her. "You're so sweet to do this," Dr. Benitez said.

"I enjoy it," Susanna replied honestly. "It's therapy for me too."

Dr. Benitez patted her arm. "How are you doing?"

"Okay, I guess." Susanna shrugged. "Some days good, some days not so good. You know?"

"I know," said Dr. Benitez.

"So, where's Danny?" asked Susanna.

"We're getting him ready for a bone marrow transplant. He's especially vulnerable to infection right now, so he has to be isolated. But he said to tell you hi."

"Tell him hi back," said Susanna.

"Will do."

The doctor returned to making her rounds. Susanna spent the next few minutes helping Becky find magazine photos for her collage, which she'd decided would be about healthy kids doing fun things *not* in a hospital.

"Getting tired of it, huh?" Susanna said sympathetically.

"I went home for Christmas, though," Becky told her, looking on the bright side.

"Good for you," Susanna said, once more biting back tears.

When she'd walked out of the cancer ward last year, Susanna had vowed never to set foot inside a hospital again. But she'd changed her mind. She didn't want to be a doctor like her mom when she grew up, didn't want to do medical research. It was her father, a painter and sculptor, who'd suggested that maybe there were other ways to deal with her grief. She'd become an art therapy volunteer, and before too long, she realized Roberto Reyes had been absolutely right, as he usually was in his quirky, intuitive way.

"If you're afraid of something, you have to look it straight in the face," he'd said. "You have to get down on the ground and wrestle with it. If you turn your back, the thing you're running away from will never stop chasing you." He'd gently brushed a tear from her cheek, his finger caked with dried clay. "It'll get easier, Suze. I promise."

Susanna was only a few years older than some of the kids in the lounge, but sometimes she felt old enough to be their grandmother. *Easier, maybe, Dad,* she thought as she cut out a picture for Becky's collage. *But never just plain easy.*

TWO

CARLY HAD TO screech to compete with the music blasting from Jason's industrial-strength stereo speakers. "Isn't this great, Suze? Aren't you having fun?"

It was ten o'clock on Friday night, and the party at Jason's was in full swing. The living room furniture had been pushed against the walls so people could dance, and that was currently the activity of choice. Jason had managed to get ahold of some beer, but he was into the designated driver thing so there was soda too.

Susanna clutched a sweating can of fruit-flavored seltzer. "Yeah," she said, because it was easier than trying to express what she was *really* feeling, which was that, as usual, it was horribly depressing to see all the people she and Seth used to hang out with together. She'd decided a while back that it was better all around to preserve an "I'm doing okay, don't worry about me" facade, even with her closest friends.

"I saw you and Jason dancing," Carly said, her tone insinuating. "You looked pretty into each other."

Susanna shrugged. It wasn't that hard to go through the motions. "The music's great. He's a good dancer."

"Did you see me talking to Anders?"

"Missed it," said Susanna. "How'd you manage to elbow your way to the front of the line?"

"You know me. I'm a steamroller." Carly tossed a glance in Anders's direction. The Norwegian boy was surrounded by girls, as he'd been all evening. "He's really, really sweet, Suze. My goal for the night is to get him to dance with me."

"I'm sure you'll have no problem."

"Probably not," Carly agreed brightly. "Know what, though? You're the one he's checking out."

Susanna raised her eyebrows. "Me? I doubt it."

"No, I swear." Carly held up her right hand, Scouts' honor fashion. "When you were with Jason before, over by the tropical fish tank."

Susanna laughed. "Are you sure he wasn't looking at the neon tetras?"

"All I'm saying is, if things don't work out with Jason, I give you permission to date Anders," Carly offered unselfishly.

Susanna was sure Anders Lund was perfectly nice as well as being as gorgeous as some kind of combination movie star and Olympic athlete, but she herself intended to give him a wide berth. In the first place, she was definitely not in the market for a boyfriend. And in the second place, a foreign exchange student was absolutely the last type of person she'd want to get involved with, since in just a few months he'd return to Norway, which was something like 10,000 miles from California. "I'm never falling in love again," Susanna said quietly, "especially not with someone who'll leave."

"What?" Carly cupped a hand to her ear. "Didn't hear you."

Susanna shook her head. "That's all right," she said, more loudly. "It was nothing."

A minute later, Carly was whisked into the whirl of dancing bodies by Brad Westerberg, a cute sophomore football player. Susanna drifted back to Jason.

He was in the middle of rehashing some locker room–oriented story with a bunch of his teammates, who were all laughing as if it were the most hilarious thing they'd ever heard. Susanna stepped next to Jason, and he slung an arm lightly around her shoulders, giving her a welcoming squeeze.

I should've stayed home, Susanna thought, a false smile pasted on her face for Jason's benefit. *I knew this would stink.* Earlier that evening, when she'd told her mother about her "date," Dr. Alison Reyes had been interested and encouraging. For some reason, her mother's upbeat response had bugged Susanna. "Why is everyone in such a hurry for me to get back to normal?" she'd burst out.

Her mother had looked at her for a long moment. "I'm sorry if I came across that way, Suze," she'd said at last. "You know you don't have to prove anything to me or your dad. Do what you feel comfortable doing."

Susanna realized now she'd been secretly hoping her mom would encourage her to skip the party, to stay home and rent a video and pig out on microwave popcorn. But that wasn't Alison Reyes's style. *She left it up to me. So here I am,* thought Susanna, *pretending the old fun-loving Susanna is back and better than ever.*

"This is a great tune," Jason said enthusiastically. "Want to dance, Susanna?"

"You bet," she replied.

I should have stayed home, Anders thought. *Why did I let Mark talk me into this?*

While he attended Altavista High, Anders was living with the Collina family, whose youngest son, Mark, was a junior. Anders and Mark had hit it off immediately—Mark's older siblings were off at college, and he seemed to enjoy having a new "brother" to hang out with. The problem was, they weren't hanging out together right now. As soon as they'd gotten to Jason's, Mark had taken off, abandoning Anders to . . .

"My turn," declared Shannon, grabbing Anders's hand and hauling him away from the other girls. "This is a *great* tune. Come on!"

Anders couldn't remember the last time he'd danced nonstop like this. He supposed it was preferable to just standing around. At least when he was dancing, he only had to deal with one girl at a time.

"You're a *great* dancer," Shannon enthused, taking advantage of the crowded room to press close to Anders. "I guess all that Nordic skiing gets you in pretty good shape, huh?"

"Well, dancing uses different muscles," Anders pointed out.

Shannon laughed. "Oh, you have the *greatest* sense of humor!"

Anders smiled amiably, even though he didn't have the faintest idea why she thought his remark was funny. American girls seemed to find everything funny. And everything was "great." He made a mental note to start using the adjective often.

After a minute or so, Anders started to unbend. Shannon was enjoying herself—they were surrounded by people having a good time. It was almost contagious. "This reminds me a little of Friday nights in Bergen," Anders told Shannon. "My friends and I go out to hear live music and dance."

"Great!" said Shannon.

When the song ended, Chelsea appeared next to them and asked Anders to dance with her. Shannon declared that Anders was still "hers" for one more song, "because Tiffany had him for two songs." The music started up again, but the girls continued to bicker. Embarrassed, Anders shuffled his feet, tempted to ditch both girls. Searching for an escape route, he found himself staring straight at the girl who was dancing with Jason.

She was slender and tall, with long, dark blond

hair and delicate features. She wore a close-fitting black top with long sleeves and a scooped neck and a very short skirt. Anders couldn't help noticing her legs. They were long and slim, but what he liked best about them was that they looked strong. *She's an athlete,* he guessed. Even more than her legs, though, he noticed her eyes. They were big and dark, and her lashes were about a foot long and . . . *She's looking right at me,* Anders realized, flushing.

Their eyes locked just long enough for Anders to catch a flash of amused sympathy, then the girl and Jason whirled off. Though they hadn't been introduced yet, Anders knew her name because he'd heard the other girls speculating about whether she and Jason were a serious item: Susanna. She was very pretty, Anders thought, and he got the impression that many of the other boys at A.H.S. concurred. Not that he was interested. He wasn't looking for a girlfriend, and certainly not the bubbly, cute, center-of-attention type. The Jennifer type.

"Sorry you had to leave your own party to drive me home," Susanna apologized to Jason.

It was only eleven-thirty. Jason's car was parked in the Reyeses' driveway, the engine idling. "No problem," he replied. "I know you've got a lot going on." His voice was low and sincere; when he looked into her eyes, Susanna could see that he understood. "Hey, we'll try again sometime."

"You bet," she said softly. "You're a good sport."

"You too, kiddo."

Susanna put her hand on the car door handle. "Let me walk you to the house," Jason offered.

"It's okay. You'd better get back to your place before it gets trashed."

Jason put a hand on her shoulder. As he leaned toward her, Susanna steeled herself for a goodnight kiss. At the last instant, she turned her face away so that his lips brushed her cheek. "'Night, Jason," she whispered, stepping quickly from the car.

"'Night, Suze," he called after her. "See you in school."

By eleven-thirty, Anders had had enough partying. Mark cheerfully tossed him the car keys, saying he could hitch a ride home with a friend. Back at the house, Mr. and Mrs. Collina were already asleep. Anders went quietly upstairs to his room, which until recently had been Mark's big brother Ben's room. Ben was a senior at an East Coast university now, but the room was still decorated with his stuff: posters, photographs, sports trophies. The few personal things Anders had brought with him from Norway—a framed picture of his family, a compass and Swiss Army knife for hiking, half a dozen paperback books including an English/Norwegian dictionary—were arranged neatly on the desk.

Anders sat at the desk and opened a small leather address book. There was a photo tucked in the front. Removing it carefully, he looked at it for a long minute. The girl in the picture was wearing a stylish, close-fitting ski outfit, and she was gorgeous, with

21

long dark curls, sparkling green eyes, and a brilliant smile. Her personality had been as dazzling as her looks. Was it any wonder he'd fallen in love with her?

Anders sighed deeply. It had been seven months since he'd last seen Jennifer Nelson in person, but the pain was still fresh. He wasn't sure he'd ever entirely get over her. She was the first girl he'd really cared for, the first to whom he'd given his heart. *And what a mistake that was,* he thought.

Jennifer had been an American exchange student at Anders's high school in Bergen the previous spring semester. The two were attracted to each other instantly—within a week, they were a couple, inseparable. When it came time for Jennifer to fly home to southern California in June, it had nearly broken Anders's heart, but she'd promised they'd find a way to be together again. Then, a week later, he got the letter.

He'd saved the letter in his address book too, folded into a tiny square. Smoothing the page out on the desk, he read it for what was probably the hundredth time. It was short, breezy, final.

Dear Anders,

There's no way to break this gently, so I'll get straight to the point. I got back together with my old boyfriend, Bill, so I don't think it would be a good idea for you and I to stay in touch. I'm sorry it had to end this way. We had a lot of fun, didn't we? I'll never forget you.

Lots of love,
Jennifer

Anders put the letter back in its crumpled envelope and started to fold it up again. Then he stopped, his gaze transfixed by the return address: 1616 Palm Court, Beverly Hills.

He hadn't planned to contact her. What was the point? To use an American expression that he found very apt, she'd dumped him. *But we're in the same country,* Anders thought. *Even the same state.* She was in southern California and he was up north, but still.

He tore a piece of paper from a notebook before he could change his mind. He wrote in English, his print neat and small, pausing only occasionally to search for the right word.

> *Hei,* Jennifer,
>   Guess who? You won't believe it, but I'm in America to study for a semester, at a really great high school in Altavista, north of the Golden Gate Bridge.

He added a few more sentences, signed his name, and wrote the Collinas' address and phone number underneath. Then he reread the letter, nodding to himself with satisfaction. It was a perfectly casual, no-hard-feelings type of letter. He didn't suggest a visit or getting back together or anything like that; he'd left the next move up to her. He'd happily settle for a phone call or even a postcard—just some sign that she remembered him and what they'd once shared.

As he sealed the envelope, though, Anders's heart was racing as if he'd just sprinted full speed up the mountain behind his family's house in Bergen. Yes, he'd settle for a friendly gesture. But deep down inside, he couldn't help hoping for something more.

Susanna hung her jacket in the hall closet and walked into the living room of her family's sprawling ranch house. Her parents were in bed, but they'd left a light on. The room was comfortably cluttered with her father's artwork—three-dimensional pieces constructed from what he called "found" materials but what most people would call junk—and stacks of her mother's medical journals. Tonight there was also a note pinned to the overstuffed sofa: "Suze—homemade brownies in the kitchen if you want a midnight snack—Mom."

Susanna removed the note, then plumped up the sofa cushion. "In the mood for a brownie?" she asked softly. She was answered by the muffled thump of Timber's tail against the rug. The shaggy, long-legged mutt sat up and smiled at her, his tongue lolling with expectation.

She wasn't hungry, but she grabbed a brownie anyway, letting Timber lick the crumbs from her fingers before heading down the hallway to her bedroom. Leaving the light off, she undressed quietly in the dark. After bundling into flannel pajamas and a pair of thick socks—her parents were big on conserving energy and refused to run the heat at

24

night, even when it was close to freezing—she pulled back the covers on her bed. Instead of crawling in, though, she wrapped herself in the down comforter and opened the drawer of her nightstand, taking out a small photo album.

Moonlight poured through her window, enabling Susanna to see the pictures inside the album clearly. They were mostly of her and Seth. He was good-looking, with bright blue eyes, a shock of dark hair falling over his forehead, and a wide, mischievous grin. Susanna turned the pages slowly, drinking in the images. The photos had been taken all over the place: sunset at Stinson Beach, skiing at Lake Tahoe, leaning against their mountain bikes on a local trail. There was one common thread: She and Seth were always smiling, always happy.

I remember this day. Susanna lingered over a picture of the two of them taken one spring on top of Half Dome in Yosemite National Park. The final part of the climb had been up cables on the sheer stone face, and she'd started to panic—but Seth had talked her through it, and she'd made it all the way. In the picture she looked a little punch-drunk, giddy from the feeling of standing on top of the world with her arms around the person she loved most in the world.

After Yosemite, there was a gap, empty pages where summer should have been. The last few photographs in the album were dramatically different from what had come before. Seth was sitting in a hospital bed, thin and pale. Even when he'd lost his hair, though, he'd still smile gamely from under the brim of his A.H.S. Ospreys baseball cap. Always smiling, right up until the end.

Susanna closed the album, holding it on her lap as she looked out her window at the bright white winter moon. They'd never made it back to Yosemite, or to Lake Tahoe, or to Stinson Beach. It had been hardest for Seth in the fall, the season he loved most. Susanna recalled one perfect October day . . . a warm, sunny afternoon cooling to a twilight flavored with the sharp, rich scent of wood smoke and fallen leaves. So beautiful, but the beauty stabbed like a knife because Seth wasn't there to share it, because that very day was his funeral. He'd lost his brief fight against cancer. He was gone.

The moon's crisp outline blurred as Susanna started to cry. Tears rolled down her cheeks, dropping silently onto the photo album's quilted cover. "I miss you, Seth," she whispered.

THREE

MONDAY MORNING BEFORE the first bell, Susanna and Carly met at their lockers as usual. "I need a pen," Susanna mumbled as she rummaged through her locker. "Can I borrow a pen? Carly? Hey, Donovan. Yoo-hoo."

Carly wasn't paying any attention. Susanna straightened up. Following her friend's gaze, she saw Brad Westerberg across the hall. Brad waved cheerfully to Carly. Carly returned the wave, her cheeks the same color as her red sweater.

When Brad had disappeared into the crowd, Susanna put her hands on her hips. "I have never in my entire life seen you blush, Ms. Donovan," she observed. "What's the story?"

Carly put her hands to her face. "Is it that obvious? Suze, you will absolutely *not* believe what happened the other night at Jason's party after you left! I positively can't believe I did this!"

"What did you do?" asked Susanna, her curiosity growing.

"Okay, it was like this." Carly gestured with her hands as she always did when she was nervous or excited. "Brad and I started talking about this TV show we both like, you know? Like, what characters we like best and how we can't stand this one character and about last week's episode that, like, totally blew both our minds."

"And, like, like, then what?" Susanna teased.

"Like, the next thing I knew, we'd been talking for like an *hour*," Carly declared. "The time just flew! I was having a blast! And there was this really weird chemistry happening between us." She lowered her voice. "Like *sparks*."

"Sparks." Susanna grinned. "Sparks are good."

"Yeah, but then he suggested going outside for some air."

"Air, huh? Very original."

"I know, I know," Carly groaned. "So we went outside, and it was, like, freezing, so he put his jacket around me and then . . . and then . . ." She gripped Susanna's arm. "We kissed," she concluded in a grim tone as if she were announcing the outbreak of war.

"Well? Was it . . . was he . . . ?" Susanna inquired delicately.

"It was fantastic," Carly admitted sadly.

"So, what's the problem?" Susanna wanted to know. "Brad's adorable. Our families are good friends—his dad's a doctor at the clinic with my mom. I think this is great!"

"It's not great, it's horrible," Carly wailed. "He's only a sophomore!"

"So?"

"A *sophomore*," Carly repeated as if Susanna were completely dense. "As in two years younger than me. Actually, only a year and three months younger," she amended. "He has an early birthday and I have a late one. But *still*."

"But still," Susanna echoed, "I don't see why—"

"I could never in a million years date a sophomore," Carly declared. "A college sophomore, yes, but not a high-school one."

"What difference does it make?" wondered Susanna. "If you like each other—"

"It would just be so uncool." Carly's tone made it clear this was the final word on the subject. "I just really hope he didn't get the wrong idea and think we're going to, like, start going out. It was just a . . . thing. One of those things. A complete mistake."

Susanna shook her head. She knew there wasn't any point in trying to change Carly's mind. *Before Seth, I used to think that kind of stuff was important too,* she recalled. *How old a guy was, whether the relationship would make me look cool.* "Too bad," she said, "because he's incredibly cute."

"Let's change the subject," Carly suggested quickly. "Let's talk about you and Jason. How'd it go?"

Susanna slammed her locker shut. "It didn't."

"I'm sorry." Carly patted Susanna on the shoulder.

"I'm not," Susanna said cheerfully. "Jason's nice—I've always thought so. But that 'sparks' thing you were talking about? It's not there with us." She didn't bother adding that she didn't expect to ever again feel sparks with any guy.

"Well, it's okay," Carly said consolingly. "There are plenty of other guys interested in you. You don't exactly have to worry about sitting home the night of our senior prom."

Susanna laughed. "I wasn't worrying. The prom is still four months away!"

"It's never too soon to start planning, though," noted Carly in all seriousness. "Who you'll go with, what you'll wear. Hair, accessories. Think yearbook photo. Senior prom is a once-in-a-lifetime event that'll be preserved for posterity, forever, in black and white. It's got to be perfect!"

Susanna laughed again. "Carly, you are too much."

The two girls started down the hall toward homeroom. "Well, Kate and Jin are all set for dates: Kate's got Doug, and Jin's got Kenny. So that just leaves you and me, and speaking for myself, I aim to snag Anders Lund," Carly pronounced. "He's currently definitely the most eligible guy at Altavista High. Can't you just see me at the prom with him?"

"Sure. Whatever you say."

They ducked into the ladies' room for a quick mirror check. "Before I got sidetracked by Brad at the party, I was talking to Anders for, like, the longest time about his interests," Carly told Susanna.

"I hope you took copious notes," Susanna kidded.

Carly whipped out a hairbrush. "I found out that he's into all these woodsy, outdoor,

Scandinavian-type things like backpacking and cross-country skiing."

"Did you confess that *you* were into indoor mall-type things like shopping and channel surfing?"

"No, I said I was a charter member of the A.H.S. Outdoors Club." Carly blinked her eyes, carefully dabbing a coat of mascara onto her thick lashes. "He's signing up for the club's next hike."

"And this affects you how?"

"Us," Carly corrected, capping the tube of mascara and sticking it back in her bag. "I signed you and me up too."

"Oh, Carly," Susanna said with a sigh. "You *hate* hiking."

"And you love it," Carly pointed out. "I need your help."

Susanna smiled, her eyes stinging suddenly with unexpected tears. "What would I do without you, Donovan? You always make me laugh."

Carly folded Susanna in a quick hug. "Hey, that's what friends are for."

"Thanks for waiting for me," Carly panted as she hauled herself up a steep section of trail.

"That's what friends are for," said Susanna. Just ahead, the rest of the group had paused for a break. Susanna got out a bottle of water and offered it to Carly. "Let's rest for a minute."

Carly appeared only too happy to dump her heavy backpack on the side of the trail. The Outdoors Club had gotten beautiful winter weather for its Saturday hike through a scenic national park near the coast. The day was windy and clear. Periodically, the trail swept out of the forest and over grassy stretches of ground with breathtaking ocean views. As Carly gulped down the water, Susanna squinted toward the horizon where the Pacific sparkled like a jewel. "The gray whales are migrating this time of year," she remarked. "Maybe we'll see some!"

"Whales, yeah, great," Carly said feebly. She wiped her mouth on her sleeve and handed the bottle back to Susanna. It was empty. "Sorry."

Susanna tucked the bottle back in her pack. "I have another bottle; I always drink tons on a long hike like this," she said pointedly. Water wasn't the only essential thing Carly had forgotten to bring—she'd already had to borrow sunscreen, Band-Aids, and a pair of dry socks from Susanna. "What's in your pack anyway?"

"My cellular phone, makeup, hairstyling mousse and gel, a portable curling iron—"

"A *curling iron?*"

"Well, I didn't know how my hair would look after a day of hiking!" Carly said indignantly. "Come on." Bending over, she hoisted her backpack with a melodramatic groan. "They're starting again. I've got to catch up with Anders!"

Privately, Susanna thought Carly had zero chance of catching up with Anders. Not that Carly was the only one lagging. There'd been a record turnout for the hike of girls like Carly who'd never been in the least bit interested in Outdoors Club activities until Anders Lund got to town. The cheerleaders were keeping up with him, though; Susanna could see Tiffany, Rachel, and Shannon sticking to the poor guy like burrs.

Carly and Susanna trudged on. "How are those boots working out?" Susanna asked her friend.

Carly looked down with disgust at her brand-new, high-tech hiking boots. "I can feel seventeen different blisters popping out on my feet. I'll need more Band-Aids in a minute."

"Well, look on the bright side," Susanna said. "The boots'll be all broken in for the next Outdoors Club hike."

"Yeah, right. Like I might ever subject myself to this torture again."

Just ahead on the path, two boys had paused to wait for them. *Oh, no,* thought Susanna. She was pretty sure Jose Martinez had a crush on her—he was always trying to sit next to her in history. And she knew Curtis Baldwin, the Outdoors Club president, liked her—he'd asked her out just the week before, but she'd told him she was busy.

The boys fell into step with Susanna and Carly. "Haven't seen you on a hike before," Curtis said meaningfully.

"To be honest, it never occurred to me to join the club because I can just walk out my front door and do this," Susanna replied, hoping he didn't assume that, like Carly, she was on the hike to meet guys, particularly guys named Curtis.

"How 'bout you, Carly? Having fun?" Curtis asked.

"Oh, I'm having a ball," Carly said dryly.

Jose managed to elbow his way past Curtis. "Isn't this a beautiful park?" he asked Susanna.

"Sure is," she agreed.

"It's historical too," Jose went on. "We're really near where Sir Francis Drake put ashore in 1579. And, of course, the native Miwok and Ohlone peoples were living here long before that. . . ."

Jose launched into an animated lecture about the archaeological significance of shell mounds and the artistry of Miwok feather baskets. Every time there was a bend in the narrow trail, he and Curtis jostled to see who'd end up walking closest to Susanna. *So much for the peace and quiet of nature,* Susanna thought with a sigh.

Anders resisted the urge to clap his hands over his ears. What was it about American girls and their apparently incessant need to talk, talk, *talk?* For a solid four miles, Rachel, Shannon, and Tiffany had chattered nonstop about every subject under the sun. They'd critiqued the outfit and hairstyle of every other girl on the hike; they'd determined that Tiffany's parents were the strictest and Shannon's were the coolest, while Rachel's family took the best vacations; and they'd debated which actors and movies *should* win Academy Awards and which *would.* In addition, Anders had learned that Sunbright Shampoo was his best bet for bringing out blond highlights; that the afternoon deejay on KFOG was giving away free Smashing Pumpkins tickets; and that, despite the claims of advertising, frozen yogurt has more calories than you'd think.

But by far their favorite topic of conversation was Anders himself. They wanted to know everything about him. His answers to their questions tended to be brief and even terse, but if anything, this only made them pry more energetically. When he was forced to admit that he didn't have a girlfriend back in Bergen, their eyes had lit up. He tried to backtrack, saying there *was* someone, sort of, only she wasn't Norwegian, but it was too late. Word was out: Anders was available.

"I've got an extra ticket for a concert at the Filmore in San Francisco Friday night," Rachel was saying. She put a hand on his arm. "Do you want to go with me, Anders?"

"I'm having a party on Saturday, Anders," Shannon piped up, taking his other arm. "I really hope you can make it."

"Have you been to the wine country yet?" asked Tiffany. Anders didn't have an arm left, so she just blinked her long eyelashes invitingly. "We could take a driving tour of Napa and Sonoma after school one day next week."

Anders's head spun. He couldn't say yes to all these girls, but they made it almost impossible to say no. "Um . . ." He stopped dead in his tracks. Unzipping his backpack, he took out a compass and map. "I will go off the trail for a while," he announced. "For practicing my *orienterings*."

"Your what?" the three girls chorused.

He started to explain. "It is a Scandinavian sport where—" Then he caught himself. This was his chance to escape, he'd better take it. "I will rejoin the group farther along," he promised, jogging off.

"Look, there goes Anders!" Carly said to Susanna. "He's taking off by himself."

Susanna shielded her eyes with her hand. "Can't say I blame him."

"I'm going to follow him," Carly declared. "Maybe he's found a shortcut."

Anders was already a tiny speck in the distance. "You'll only get lost," Susanna warned.

Carly wasn't worried. "So I get lost. I'll be with Anders—how bad could it be?"

She set off blithely across the meadow in the direction Anders had taken. Susanna watched for a minute, biting her lip. Then she trotted after her friend. "Wait up!" she called.

An hour later, the two girls were slogging their way through a marshy bog choked with scratchy underbrush. Susanna was lugging Carly's backpack as well as her own.

Carly was limping from her blisters. "Why on earth did Anders come this way?" she wondered petulantly as she stepped on a flat, sturdy-looking rock. She screeched as the rock sank under her weight, leaving her ankle-deep in cold mud.

"We don't know that he did," Susanna pointed

out, plucking a spiky branch from the sleeve of her fleece pullover. "We have no idea where Anders went or where the rest of the club is either."

"So you're saying we're lost."

"Mountain lion bait," Susanna confirmed.

"Terrific," Carly moaned. "You're supposed to be such a hotshot nature girl, Suze. How could you get us lost?"

"So now *I'm* responsible?" Susanna retorted. "It was your brilliant idea to leave the trail!"

"Well, I'm tired and hungry," Carly complained, "and my feet hurt and—" She stopped, her eyes brightening. "We're saved!" she exclaimed, pointing.

Ahead of them, on top of a high bluff, a lone figure was silhouetted against the sky. Susanna suppressed a giggle. *Wouldn't you know,* she thought. *Mr. Universe!*

"Anders!" Carly shrieked, waving her arms like crazy. "Anders, over here!"

Anders turned. He waved in recognition, then hiked down the hill. "Boy, are we glad to see you!" Carly cried when he reached them. "We were starting to think we'd never find our way back to the group."

"They are just over that rise," Anders told her, gesturing to the bluff. "Come on. I will guide you."

Carly had finally ambushed Anders, but before she could say another word to him, he set off with long strides. Susanna kept pace with him easily, but Carly soon fell behind, limping and huffing, a grumpy expression on her face. *I don't think this is the romantic stroll she was shooting for!* Susanna thought, still trying not to grin.

For a few minutes, Anders maintained an aloof silence, occasionally shooting a wary glance at Susanna out of the corner of his eye as if he thought she were about to pounce on him. Finally, when she didn't speak, he pointed to her doubled-up backpacks. "May I help you carry some of that gear?"

"I can handle it," Susanna assured him cheerfully. "Thanks anyway."

They hiked on without further conversation. Gradually, Anders seemed to relax. At one point, he even smiled at her, a shy, grateful expression flickering in his light blue eyes. Covertly, Susanna took a closer look at him. He was definitely handsome, with a thin, interestingly angular face. She glimpsed an understated charm too, but he was first and foremost the silent, stoic type. *Dealing with Tiffany and Company must be torture for him,* Susanna guessed. He was clearly relieved that Susanna wasn't trying to flirt with him and that Carly was too tired to. The poor guy.

The rest of the Outdoors Club was waiting for them on the rocky beach, already digging into their picnic lunches. "Food," Carly exclaimed, her eyes glazing over. "I've never been so hungry in my life."

"I'm psyched for a break," Susanna agreed, dropping the backpacks onto a flat stone.

"Just a break?" Carly turned pale under her windburn. "You mean this isn't the end of the hike?"

"Of course not, silly. We're only half the way. We have to hike back to the parking lot."

Carly collapsed in a heap. "I won't survive," she groaned. She unlaced one of her hiking boots and gingerly massaged her foot. "I had no idea trying to impress a Norwegian was going to be so brutal."

"So don't," suggested Susanna, lobbing a box of raisins at her friend. "Go for it with Brad Westerberg who likes you just the way you are."

Carly shook her head, stubborn. "I'll just have to work out every day to get in better shape. You'll go to the gym with me, won't you, Suze?"

Susanna laughed. "I have a feeling this is going to be an exhausting winter!"

FOUR

"So, I heard Rivers struck out with Reyes," Mark Collina said conversationally to Rich Danson, his seatmate on the charter bus to Lake Tahoe.

"She went out with him once, but nothing came of it," Rich confirmed.

"I heard Austin Jenner asked her out too," put in Antonio Nuñez from the seat in front of Mark and Rich. "Supposedly, she gave him the ol' 'Sorry, I'll be busy washing my hair on Saturday night.'"

Anders was sitting next to Antonio. The four boys, plus a few dozen other A.H.S. students, were heading east on Interstate 80. The Outdoors Club had sponsored a day of cross-country skiing in the Sierra Nevada mountains. Waiting for the bus that morning, Anders had, once again, been besieged by aggressively hopeful girls. He'd managed to dive into the empty seat next to Antonio, narrowly escaping the torture of two and a half hours in a confined space with Shannon or Alicia.

For once, safely surrounded by guys slouched in their seats slurping coffee from thermoses and munching trail mix, Anders felt as if he could relax and be himself. "Reyes?" he said, folding his long legs in half and propping his knees against the back of the seat in front of him. He was pretty sure they were talking about the girl he'd noticed at Jason Rivers's party and then spoken to briefly on the Outdoors Club hike two weekends ago. She was on the bus today too—way up front with her flirty friend Carly, while he and the guys were in the back. "You mean Susanna? The blonde?"

"Yep," said Mark. "You've met her?"

Anders nodded. "She is . . ." He fished around in his brain for the correct English word. "Popular. Yes?"

"Affirmative," said Rich.

"I don't know," put in Tim Epstein from two rows behind Anders. Tim leaned forward, his arms folded on the back of Mark's seat. "I think people should give her more space. It hasn't been *that* long since, you know, Seth."

The other guys, with the exception of Anders, all nodded thoughtfully, their expressions suddenly somber. "Who is Seth?" Anders asked.

"Who *was* Seth, you mean," Rich said, a tinge of sadness in his voice.

Anders rephrased the question. "Who was Seth?"

"Seth and Susanna used to go out," Antonio informed Anders. "But Seth got cancer. He died last fall."

Anders pictured Susanna Reyes. She'd caught his eye that night at Jason's party, but only because she was extremely pretty. On the hike, though, he'd formed a different impression of her. She'd struck him then as independent, friendly but not too friendly, and somehow—though she clearly was "popular"—*apart.* "I see," Anders said quietly.

"So, like, a lot of guys have been wondering what the etiquette is in bereavement-type situations like this," Rich explained to Anders. "Like, how long do you have to wait if you want to ask her out. What's the conventional wisdom in Norway?"

Anders shook his head. "I don't know what I would do," he admitted.

"Wait longer," Mark declared. "I'd give her a little more time."

"She's gotta get over it, though," reasoned Antonio.

"Wish she'd get over it with me," said Rich.

"It's still too soon," Tim concluded.

The guys moved on to a discussion of whether snowboarding was more fun than downhill skiing or whether it was just that the clothes were cooler. Anders continued to think about Susanna Reyes. He pictured her delicately beautiful face and the wide smile that didn't quite reach her eyes. *Tim is right,* Anders thought. *It is still too soon.*

"Maybe we should just go back to the lodge," Susanna said with an exasperated sigh, wishing she hadn't allowed Carly to talk her into coming with her on another Outdoors Club trip.

Carly was a disaster waiting to happen, even more helpless on skis than she'd been in hiking boots. With Anders leading the way, the rest of the group had sped off down the scenic trail. Meanwhile, Carly floundered in the soft snow, unable to go more than a few feet without crossing the tips of her skis and toppling over sideways.

At the moment, she was lying flat on her back in the powder, catching her breath after a particularly spectacular fall. "I just haven't gotten my rhythm yet," she responded as Susanna hauled her back onto her feet and helped her retrieve her poles. "I'm sure I'll get the hang of it soon."

"Yeah, just in time for us to get back on the bus," Susanna grumbled.

"What?" asked Carly.

Susanna took a deep breath of cold, fresh mountain air. She was itching to whiz along the snowy trails with the others, but she couldn't exactly leave Carly behind making snow angels. "Nothing," she said, managing a smile. "I'm sure you will get the hang of it. Just pretend you're on one of those machines at the gym, okay?"

They moved forward, Carly cautiously sliding her skis along the tracks other skiers had made, her balance precarious. At the top of a gentle incline, she came to a wobbly stop. "Oh, no. A downhill!" she squeaked, terror in her voice. "What do I do?"

Susanna had zoomed ahead. She looked back up the slope at Carly. "Nothing to it," she promised. "Just coast."

Carly looked dubious. "What if I go too fast? What if I crash? What if I—"

Just then, Brad Westerberg emerged from a

stand of Douglas fir. He'd started off with the rest of the group, then doubled back. "Like this, Carly," he called to her, demonstrating. "Keep your skis parallel and center yourself over them. Now, bend your knees a little and lean forward just slightly." He flashed her an encouraging grin. "And relax, would you? This is supposed to be fun!"

Carly laughed breathlessly. "Yeah, right!"

Following his instructions, Carly slid forward down the incline. Her arms windmilled as she picked up speed, but miraculously, she managed to keep her balance. Susanna clapped her gloved hands. "Bravo!" she cheered.

Carly beamed. "Told you I could do it." She smiled gratefully at Brad. "You're a good coach."

"Yeah, well . . ." He shrugged, looking pleased.

The three skied off, with Carly in between Susanna and Brad while Brad periodically called out tips. They covered about a mile, and Carly fell only once. Susanna was starting to think the ski trip wouldn't be ruined after all.

Then Carly called out, "Look, I can see Lake Tahoe!" She twisted at the waist, waving her ski pole toward the lake, but the movement caused her to lose her balance. For a few seconds, she swayed dramatically from side to side, trying to steady herself. She ended up sailing down a hill, her arms flailing, just as Anders and some others reappeared on the trail ahead of them. *"Heeeellpp!"* Carly screeched.

One of her skis must have hit a root or stone, because suddenly, she launched into the air like a missile. An instant later, she landed in the snow, a tangled heap of arms, legs, skis, and poles. "Ouch," said Susanna with a wince.

She and Brad hurried to Carly's side. Anders reached her first. Carly was sitting up, one leg folded underneath her, her hair covered with snow and tears streaking her face. "I think I broke my ankle," she moaned.

"Sit still and catch your breath," Anders advised. He studied the position of her leg, then peered into her eyes. "Your pain doesn't seem to be that intense," he observed. "You're not in shock."

"I guess not," Carly agreed tremulously.

"Can you move at all?" Anders asked.

"Careful," Brad interjected.

Carly straightened her bent leg. "It hurts," she said, biting back a sob.

Anders looked at her ankle. "I don't think it is broken, but it might be sprained."

"I'll ski back to the lodge and get help," Brad offered.

Anders shook his head. "That will take too long. I'll carry her."

Before Carly could protest, Anders bent over and scooped her up. As he skied off, not slowed down in the least by his burden, Susanna noticed that Carly, despite her pain, looked pretty happy to be in Anders's arms. "Unbelievable," Susanna marveled as she followed them back toward the lodge. "Absolutely unbelievable!"

Carly sat in front of the fireplace in the lodge, her bandaged ankle elevated on a stool. "Guess I won't be skiing any more this afternoon."

"You won't be skiing any more this *year*," Susanna corrected.

"You know, you don't have to stay in here with me," Carly said to Anders. She fluttered her eyelashes. "I totally understand if you want to get back out in the snow."

Brad stepped forward. "Yeah, you go on, Anders. I'll keep Carly comfortable."

Anders had been pacing restlessly. Now he practically bolted for the door. "Okay," he said. "Great. See you."

Susanna watched him go, as Carly pouted with disappointment. Clearly, she hadn't expected him to be quite so eager to escape.

"Can I get you some hot chocolate?" Brad asked her. "Or how about a sandwich?"

"If you can't ski, you might as well enjoy yourself in here, Carly," Susanna pointed out.

"Well . . ." Carly shrugged. "Yeah, sure. Thanks."

Five minutes later, Carly and Brad were sipping hot chocolate and sharing a chili dog and a basket of french fries while Brad made Carly laugh by telling stories about when he'd learned to ski. It was pretty clear that her friend wasn't going to be lonely, so Susanna headed back out to the ski trails.

Rays of afternoon sunshine slanted through the trees, casting long blue shadows on the snow. The air was still and pure. And something about the smell of pine needles . . .

The memory took Susanna by surprise, washing

over her with an almost physical intensity. She and Seth had gone downhill skiing on a day a lot like this, before he got sick. They were riding up the chairlift together, and just as they passed a tall stand of pines, the trees' branches heaped with fluffy snow, Seth had turned to her and pushed her goggles up on her head so he could kiss her. The memory was so vivid, she could almost reach out and touch him.

Tears stung Susanna's eyes. She blinked them away, focusing again on the real world. Her feet and hands were growing cold—she needed to get moving. But suddenly, skiing alone didn't seem like that much fun. *I could go back inside and hang out with Carly and Brad,* she thought. *Nah, they don't need me.* It occurred to her that she could have asked Anders to wait so that they could ski together. Too late now—he was long gone.

Susanna pushed off with her poles, gliding effortlessly down the trail. *Look at the bright side,* she thought. *Skiing by myself beats skiing with Jose and Curtis!* Even so, she couldn't prevent a few more hot tears from spilling down her face and plopping into the snow. The ache inside her heart was just too sharp. She longed for Carly's frivolous chatter—anything to distract her from thinking about the fact that she'd never see or touch or talk to or ski with Seth again.

"I'm giving up on Anders," Carly reported to Susanna on the phone a few days later.

"Oh, really?" Susanna said teasingly. "Why?"

"Because it's *dangerous* chasing after a guy like that! Thanks to him, I'm on crutches for two weeks!"

Susanna opted not to argue with her friend's logic. "How about Brad? You two were pretty snuggly on the bus ride home from the ski trip."

"Brad's a sweetheart, but I totally think of him as a brother. A *younger* brother," Carly emphasized.

"Whatever you say." Susanna looked out her bedroom window. Rain dripped steadily down the glass pane. "Hey, want to go to a movie?"

"I'm working on that Community Service Club scholarship application," Carly replied. "You should be too."

"I know." Susanna sighed. "Okay. See ya."

"Be ya."

Susanna was just replacing the receiver when the phone rang again right under her hand. "Hello?" she said.

"Is Susanna . . . I mean, may I, uh, speak to, uh, Susanna?" a nervous male voice asked.

"You may and you are."

"Susanna, it's, uh, Peter. Peter Howe. From your biology class."

Peter Howe. Susanna wrinkled her forehead, trying to picture him. She was pretty sure his lab station was on the opposite side of the room from hers. *Tall with a zillion freckles,* she thought. *Always wears a black turtleneck even when it's ninety degrees.* "Sure, Peter," she said. "What's up?"

"Uh, well, I'm calling because . . . I know it's a long way off, but I thought maybe I'd have a better chance if . . ." She heard him gulp. "The prom," he choked out at last. "Would you . . . do you think you might—I know a lot of guys will probably ask you but—be my date?"

Susanna's fingers tightened on the phone. She wasn't that surprised to get a call from a guy like Peter. But the prom . . .

Her throat felt tight and dry. She and Seth had gone to the last prom together, and it had been the most romantic night of Susanna's life. In a million years, it would never have occurred to her then that Seth wouldn't be around to be her date for the senior prom too. To be her date for the rest of her life.

"Peter, that's a very sweet invitation, and I'm flattered," Susanna said, recovering her composure enough to be superficially polite. "But at this point, I'm not sure I even want to go to the dance. So in fairness to you, I'll have to say no. Thanks, though."

Peter stuttered a little bit more, and then they said good-bye. *Phew!* Susanna thought as she hung up the phone.

The two-page Community Service Club scholarship application was buried under some other papers on her desk. Digging it out, Susanna flipped through it halfheartedly. The easy stuff was already done—filling out her name and address, listing her extracurricular activities, forwarding her test scores, and requesting teacher recommendations—but she hadn't made much progress on the essay. She'd had the same problem getting motivated to do her college applications last fall. A year ago, she might have gotten excited about the whole process. She and

Seth used to talk all the time about going to Harvard or Princeton together—she'd be pre-med and he'd study environmental science. Now Susanna really didn't care where she ended up going to college, much less whether or not she won a scholarship.

Outside, rain continued to fall. The gray sky matched Susanna's mood. When the phone rang again, she picked it up quickly, hoping it was Carly saying she wanted to go to a matinee after all.

Someone wanted to go to a movie all right, but it wasn't Carly. "I really can't, Curtis. Thanks anyway," Susanna said politely. "I've got to get this scholarship application finished, you know?"

She turned off the ringer on her phone. She wasn't up for any more phone calls, especially from guys asking her out. Picking up a pen, she wrote "C.S.C. essay" at the top of a blank sheet of paper. *What to write about,* Susanna mused. *Volunteering at the hospital? Being captain of the A.H.S. softball team? Being part of a multicultural family with relatives in Mexico and all that jazz?*

She doodled for a minute: a tree with gnarled branches, a tightly closed rosebud, a tornado. Not a single word emerged from her brain, though. For months, she'd worn a mask, put on an act, so she wouldn't be a downer around her friends, who all missed Seth almost as much as she did. Now it was as if she'd bottled herself up for so long that her real personality had completely disappeared. She was mute.

Unable to sit still any longer, Susanna pushed back her chair and bolted from her room. Her father's studio was attached to the house by a breezeway. Wandering out there, she peeked through the half-open door. Roberto Reyes was sculpting—in high gear, totally energized, wholly focused on his work. When he caught sight of his daughter, he tossed her a wave, but she could tell he didn't want to be interrupted.

As Susanna turned back to the main house, she suddenly realized that wet weather or not, she couldn't bear to stay inside another minute. Grabbing a bright yellow slicker from the coat closet, she whistled for the dog. "Come on, Timber," she called. "Let's go for a walk."

Anders hung up the telephone in the Collinas' kitchen. He could tell his face was red—it radiated heat—but he was getting better at dealing with these calls. Alicia had just asked him to a movie at the local cinema, and Tiffany had phoned ten minutes earlier with a similar invitation. He still didn't feel good about saying no, but he didn't want to lead anybody on. It just wasn't polite.

"Was that really Tiffany Stone on the phone just now?" Mark Collina asked as he shuffled into the kitchen and grabbed an orange from the fruit bowl.

"Yes," Anders said.

"And you blew her off." Mark shook his head in amazement. "What, she's not your type?"

Anders shrugged. "No. I guess not."

Mark popped a section of orange into his mouth, still looking stumped. "Man, you really *are* foreign," he concluded.

Alone again, Anders tore into a loaf of fresh sourdough bread he'd bought at the bakery on his way home from school and chewed it thoughtfully. The attention from the girls at Altavista High was getting a little embarrassing. He sure didn't have to deal with anything like it at home. In Bergen, he was just one of the guys, well liked but not considered extraordinary. Though Jennifer had singled him out. . . .

A frown creased Anders's forehead as he stuffed the rest of the bread back in its paper bag. Jennifer. Why had he written her that stupid letter? A month had passed, but every time the phone rang, he still expected it to be her; and every time he was bitterly disappointed. It was time to face facts: He wasn't going to hear from her. He'd been an absolute fool, a *tosk,* to get his hopes up.

Anders looked out the window over the kitchen sink. It was raining steadily, as it had been for a couple of days. Good weather for moping, but moping wasn't his style. Instead, Anders did what he always did, rain or shine, when he was unhappy or mad or frustrated: He laced up his earth-stained hiking boots, shrugged into a weatherproof anorak, grabbed his backpack, and headed for the woods.

The big state park a half mile from Susanna's house was her favorite place to walk with Timber or ride her mountain bike. She usually hiked up Wildcat Canyon Trail because she loved the dramatic view from the ridge, but today, she opted to stay below in the valley, which was more protected from the wind and rain.

She tramped along the trail, her boots crunching fallen leaves. Taking deep breaths of cold, clean air spiced with the scent of wet earth and pine needles, she could almost feel her brain gradually emptying out all its crazy, confused thoughts. Timber zigzagged back and forth in front of her, happily snuffling up the interesting wild animal smells of the woods, his tail waving nonstop.

Susanna spotted the deer first. It was a buck, with a full rack of antlers—a rare sight. She stopped and stood quietly, watching the buck watch Timber. Then the dog caught a whiff of deer. "Timber, stay," Susanna commanded, lunging for Timber's collar, but it was too late. There was a flash of white as the buck turned tail and bounded off into the trees. With a howl of delight, Timber followed at full speed.

"Get back here, Timber!" Susanna hollered, running after him. She wasn't worried that Timber would actually catch up with the deer, but the park had strict rules about keeping dogs on leashes. She'd thought it was safe to let Timber run loose on a deserted, rainy day, but knowing her luck, they'd get busted by a ranger. "Timber, come!"

There was a lot of rustling and crashing as Timber galloped through the underbrush, and Susanna made a lot of noise herself. After a minute or two, though, when she stopped to catch her breath, she realized that the woods were quiet except for the drip of rain. She couldn't see or hear the dog. "Timber?" she called. She waited, listening. "Timber, I'll give you a cookie," she promised. Putting her fingers to her mouth, she whistled shrilly. "Timber!"

The woods remained still. "Fine," Susanna declared. "Be that way." Timber would just have to find his way back to her when he was ready.

Turning, Susanna started to retrace her steps. After a hundred yards or so, she paused. "This doesn't look right," she murmured to herself. "I don't remember that dead tree." She knew the park well, but she'd strayed a long way from the marked trail. Pivoting on her heel, she eyed the forest, looking for clues. Off to the right she spied some trampled ferns. *I bet Timber and I did that. The trail must be over there.*

She hiked along until she came to a little burbling creek. She definitely hadn't crossed water before . . . or did she jump the creek without even noticing it?

Susanna tilted her head back, looking up into the canopy of tree branches. The valley trail ran roughly north to south, and Timber had taken off to the left, which was west. But she had no idea which direction she was heading in now. She couldn't use the sun to orient herself because the sky was completely overcast.

Digging her hands deep into the pockets of her slicker, Susanna stared into the woods, dismayed. No two ways about it—she was lost.

FIVE

SUSANNA WALKED THROUGH the forest, occasionally clapping her hands and whistling for Timber. She could still see her way, but soon it would be pitch-dark. "Boy, are you in trouble," she warned her missing dog. "Wait'll I get my hands on you!"

The rain had stopped, but it was cold. Susanna's stomach grumbled with hunger. She considered sitting down on a log and eating the slightly smushed granola bar she'd discovered in the pocket of her coat, then decided to save it. *Hadn't planned to go camping,* she thought wryly, *or I'd have brought a bag of marshmallows!*

Since there was a decent chance she might accidentally stumble back onto the trail, she kept moving forward and tried not to panic. What was the worst thing that could happen? She'd spend the night outdoors. It wasn't *that* cold—she wouldn't get hypothermia or anything—and the park wasn't *that* big. She'd be sure to find her way out in the morning when it was light. *Mom and Dad'll form a search party,* Susanna reassured herself. *Maybe they'll send some of those rescue dogs after me. The smart kind, not idiot dogs like Timber.*

What about Timber anyhow? *Bet he ran straight home and is chowing down a bowl of kibble at this very moment,* Susanna guessed. *Or maybe—* Just ahead, a twig cracked sharply. She froze, visions of mountain lions, the kind that gobbled up stray dogs and hikers, flashing through her mind. A shadowy figure emerged from behind a tree. Too tall to be a mountain lion . . . *A bear!* Susanna thought, letting out a squeak of fear.

As the shadow came closer, she saw that it wasn't a bear, unless of course bears had wavy brown hair and wore hiking boots, faded jeans, and hunter green anoraks and navigated their way through the forest with the help of terrain maps and compasses. "Anders!" Susanna gasped, her knees crumpling with relief. "Boy, am I glad to see you!"

Anders gaped at her. "Susanna! *Hva gjør du her?* What are you doing here?"

Susanna burst out laughing. Suddenly, the situation seemed utterly Carlyesque and hilarious. "Oh, gosh, I know how this must look," she said, wiping tears from her eyes. "Here I am, right? A helpless female lost in the woods, waiting to be rescued by Anders the Norwegian superman!"

Anders grinned. "You mean, this was not arranged?"

"I swear." She crossed her heart. "I'm just out for an innocent walk with my dog."

Anders raised his eyebrows quizzically. "What dog?"

Susanna started giggling again. "I really do have a dog," she promised. "But he took off after a deer, so I ran after him and——"

As if on cue, there was a crashing in the under-brush. Timber reappeared, panting and pleased with himself. "You bad, bad dog," Susanna said, not at all sternly, as she squatted down to rub his ears. "This is Timber," she told Anders.

"*Hallo,* Timber," said Anders.

"But what about you?" she asked, flicking a damp strand of hair out of her eyes and smiling up at him. "What are you doing out in this horrible weather?"

Anders smiled sheepishly back at her. "I do not think it is so horrible. This is what it is like every day in Bergen in the summer. I am having . . . *hjemlengsel.*" He snapped his fingers. "How do you say in English? Sick for the house?"

"Homesickness." They both laughed. "Well, I'm not proud," Susanna said. "I'd be thrilled if you'd rescue me. Can you find the way out of here?"

"No problem." He pointed. "The trail's right over there. We're only a few hundred meters from the park entrance."

Susanna grinned at how close she'd been. "Then let's go."

They started off. After just a few steps, Susanna stopped abruptly. "Forgot something." Bending, she quickly snapped the leash on to Timber's collar. "You're not going anywhere, mutt," she declared. "I've had enough adventure for one day!"

Anders, Susanna, and Timber hiked along the side of the road that led to Susanna's house. Overhead, the rain clouds had parted in time for the last rays of the setting sun to paint the western sky a brilliant orange and purple. Anders and Susanna were too busy talking to notice, though.

"Altavista High, it is very different from my school back home," Anders was telling Susanna. "In the U.S. you have many more of the things to do after school, the extra—extra—"

"Extracurricular activities?"

"Yes, thanks," he said. "Sports teams, music, the clubs—we don't have that in Norway. Secondary school is just plain academics."

"But Norwegians seem really healthy and athletic," Susanna said. "Maybe you don't have organized sports at school, but you're probably more active than Americans."

"That is true," Anders agreed. "I play in a soccer league with my friends. And everybody hikes and skis, even the littlest children. As soon as they can walk!"

"So, do you like doing the club stuff at A.H.S.?" Susanna asked him. "Like the Outdoors Club trips?" A smile teased the corners of her mouth. "I mean, apart from the predatory female factor."

"There are a lot of girls in the Outdoors Club,"

Anders responded, although he wasn't sure what "predatory" meant.

"More than there used to be," she agreed.

"But, yes," Anders said. "I like the clubs. I meet people that way. Although, even meeting a lot of people, I have still felt lonely in Altavista. Until today."

He blushed. He hadn't meant to make such a personal confession. But she was so easy to talk to, it just slipped out. He shot an embarrassed glance at her. She looked straight back at him with a curious, friendly expression in her eyes. "It must be weird to be a foreigner," she remarked. "I've never been one. I mean, I've gone to Canada and Mexico, but they're not really foreign countries to me because I have relatives there."

"It is weird sometimes," he agreed, "but it is exciting too. There is so much to learn."

Susanna stopped, gesturing to a mailbox on top of a crooked post. "This is my house. Do you want a ride to the Collinas'? I'd be happy to drive you."

"It's less than a mile. I like to walk."

She smiled. "You sure do."

They stood for a moment, just looking at each other. The sun had set; it was almost dark. "I had really fun," Anders burst out suddenly. "I mean, I really . . . it was great."

"I had fun too," Susanna said sincerely.

"Because of having a conversation with a girl where it seemed like you were talking to *me* instead of . . ." He hesitated, not sure how to express himself.

"Flirting?" she supplied. "Yeah, I know what

you mean. It's good to just plain talk now and then, without playing games."

Anders grinned, happy to be understood. "Yes. Good-bye, Susanna."

She started to head down the driveway, then turned back as if on impulse. "Have you tried mountain biking yet, Anders?" she asked.

He shook his head. "No. It is a fun sport?"

"I ride all the time. Look, we have a spare bike. If it's not raining tomorrow, want to try it out?"

"Yes," he said. "I would."

"Great." She waved. "So long."

She disappeared into the dusk. Anders waited until he heard the door to her house slam, then continued along the road. He'd covered a lot of miles that afternoon, but his step was light. He felt refreshed. It was the effect of outdoor exercise, but it was something else too. *Susanna,* Anders thought.

Every now and then a group of guys from the high school invited him to hang out and shoot hoops or play video games. They were nice enough, but Anders couldn't say he'd made a real connection with any of them. They just didn't have a lot in common, and not only because Anders was foreign. *With Susanna, it was different. I've made my first real friend in Altavista,* Anders thought. And there was something else special about the last few hours. He hadn't thought about Jennifer Nelson once.

Susanna's parents were in the kitchen, debating whether to use *anchos* or *pasillas* in the *carne con chile colorado.* Susanna called hello on her way down the hall to the bathroom. Turning on the shower, she quickly stripped off her layers of clothing, then jumped in, shivering with pleasure as the hot water coursed down her cold, tired limbs.

Fifteen minutes later, warmly wrapped in a thick terry-cloth robe, she sat down at the desk in her bedroom. Supper wouldn't be ready for an hour or more—the chili had to simmer. She had a good chunk of time to work on her scholarship application.

And suddenly, she actually felt as if she had something to say. The walk in the woods had loosened her up. *And bumping into Anders,* Susanna thought, smiling to herself. What a nice guy! Too bad the other girls at A.H.S. were too smitten by his gorgeous Scandinavian looks to realize that he also happened to be sweet, unpretentious, and funny.

" 'Discuss an experience or relationship that has impacted the direction you're taking toward college and a career,' " Susanna murmured, reading the essay question aloud.

She thought for a moment, then uncapped her pen and began writing.

> Danny Ingersoll is eight years old. You'd think, given our age difference, that he'd have more to learn from me than I would from him. You'd think, since he has leukemia and I'm healthy, that I'd be stronger. But it's the other way around. My mother's a doctor, and ever since I was a kid

I've always assumed I'd become a doctor too. But until I met Danny, I didn't know what healing was really all about.

Susanna wrote without pausing until dinner-time. Before heading to the kitchen, she changed into leggings and a sweatshirt and then read over the essay. *It works,* she thought with satisfaction. It had come straight from the heart and really captured her feelings about volunteering at the hospital, her feelings about Danny and the other children.

"I can't believe I was stuck on this," she said to herself as she dropped the essay back onto her desk. She wasn't sure where this new energy and peace of mind came from, but she welcomed it. She hadn't felt this good in a long time.

SIX

"I THINK THIS is my favorite spot in all of Altavista," Susanna told Anders.

They'd met at her house after school and then mountain biked through the state park up Wildcat Canyon Trail. From the grassy meadow on top of the ridge, they could see for miles. To the west, beyond the coastal mountain range, the Pacific Ocean glittered. Over another ridge of hills to the east lay the lush green vineyards of the Sonoma Valley.

"I guess I just love the feeling of being on top of the world," Susanna explained.

"Me too." Anders leaned against his bike, contemplating the view. "There is a mountain like this behind my family's house in Bergen."

Susanna tried to picture it. "A mountain right in a city?"

"Seven mountains, actually," Anders said. "They circle the city. You can ride a tram to the top. But the center of Bergen is down at sea level. There is a harbor with very old houses, from the twelfth century, I think."

They climbed back on their bikes. The trail was wide enough to peddle side by side. "It sounds beautiful," Susanna remarked.

"It is."

She glanced at him. "Are you 'sick for the house'?"

Anders chuckled. "Homesick? No. Not today."

They biked for a while without talking. Although they still didn't know each other that well, the silence was companionable. Susanna felt entirely at ease around Anders. *He's so open and straightforward,* she thought. *He doesn't expect anything from me. There's no hidden agenda.*

"Tell me about your family," she said as they headed downhill again, their bikes bumping on the rutted dirt path.

"My father works for the city government, and my mother is a teacher," Anders told her. "I have a younger brother, Fridtjof, and a younger sister, Silje."

Susanna laughed as she tried to pronounce the names. "Fritt-juff and Sill-ya?"

"Close enough," Anders said with a grin. "And you? Do you have brothers and sisters?"

"Two older sisters in college," Susanna replied. "Angie's at Berkeley. Maria's at Harvard."

"Do you miss them?"

Susanna remembered the fall Seth had died, how empty everything seemed—her house, the whole world. She'd always had a good relationship with Seth's parents, but after Seth was gone, she couldn't bear to be with them. Since they both traveled frequently for work, avoiding them wasn't hard. Her own parents were supportive, but it was easier to talk to her sisters. Angie was local, so she'd come home as often as she could. It wasn't the same as having her there all the time, though, right in the next bedroom. "Sometimes," Susanna admitted.

She led Anders home by a different route. Half a mile from town on the quiet back road, Susanna spotted the old stucco church with the brightly painted picket fence. She'd tied a bunch of daisies to the back of her bike in case she felt like stopping.

She hesitated for a few seconds, then applied her brakes, calling over her shoulder, "Anders, let's pull in here for a minute."

Anders parked his bike and followed Susanna into the cemetery. The grass was springy under their feet, bright green from the winter rains. When she reached the white stone that marked Seth's grave, Susanna bent and gently placed the flowers there.

Though Anders was maintaining a respectful silence, Susanna felt it was only fair to enlighten him somewhat. "Seth was my . . . my boyfriend."

"I know. I'm sorry," Anders said.

He didn't press her with questions. He simply stood quietly by her side. But suddenly, Susanna felt the need to talk. "He had cancer," she told Anders. "A brain tumor. They couldn't operate on it. They did chemo and radiation but . . ." She shrugged.

"It must have been very hard for you."

"It was just so . . . fast. One day someone's with you, and the next . . ." She bit her lip.

"I understand," Anders said, his eyes sympathetic.

She sensed that somehow he did. Together they walked back to the bikes. "Seth was really great. You'd have liked him," Susanna told Anders. *And he'd have liked you,* she added to herself.

"What I think is cool about California is that there is so much variety," Anders said to Susanna a week later.

It was a sunny afternoon, unexpectedly mild, and they were walking along Stinson Beach. "It's true," agreed Susanna, tossing a stick into the waves for Timber. The dog splashed into the cold water, barking happily. "There are beaches, redwood forests, mountains, farmland."

"But the people too," said Anders. "In Norway, the people are alike, but here, in America, you have—" He looked to her for the word.

"Diversity? Yep," Susanna agreed. "I'm a case in point. I've got a little of everything in my family tree: Irish, Mexican, French, Swedish, you name it."

Anders smiled at her. "It's a nice combination."

"Thanks."

Coming upon a large, flat rock in a sheltered cove, they decided to take a break. Susanna sat down and rummaged in her backpack, pulling out a water bottle and some fruit. She tossed an apple to Anders. "What are some of the other differences you've noticed between the U.S. and Norway?"

"The biggest one is the size," Anders replied after taking a bite of the apple. "The U.S. is so enormous and powerful. That affects how Americans see themselves and the rest of the world. Considering that most of you come from immigrants, you do not know much about other cultures."

"True," Susanna conceded as she peeled an orange. "We figure everybody else knows what *we're* all about—you know, McDonald's, the Gap, Hollywood—and that's enough."

"I'm not criticizing," Anders said. "I'm here, aren't I? Everyone wants to come to America, to be like Americans. You have so much wealth and space and freedom. Endless opportunities for people to work, learn, invent, explore."

"Wait a minute. Now you sound like the tourism bureau. 'Welcome to Disneyland.' America has problems too. Crime, poverty, pollution . . ."

"Definitely," said Anders. "American society is much more violent and unequal and wasteful than Norway's. But . . ." He gestured at the deserted beach. A gull swooped down to the water's edge, plucking a crab from the foam. "Right now, right here, it is clean and peaceful."

Susanna finished her orange, then stretched out on the rock, tilting her face to the low winter sun. She sighed with contentment. "You've got that right."

They were quiet for a moment, then Anders remarked, "There is more the same than different between my country and this one."

"Yeah?"

"People are basically the same."

She sat up and smiled at him. "You mean, you have girls like Shannon and Chelsea in Bergen?"

Anders grinned. "Sure. Only, at my school, they chase after the *American* exchange students."

"So, you must have a girlfriend back home," Susanna surmised. "That's what everyone thinks. Tiffany figures it's the only explanation for why you're not swooning over her." When Anders didn't respond right away, Susanna regretted her teasing tone. "I didn't mean to be nosy. It's none of my business."

"That's okay. It's not a secret—I don't mind telling you." Anders looped his arms around his knees and gazed out at the ocean. "I don't have a girlfriend right now, but I did for a while last year."

He told Susanna the whole story of Jennifer Nelson. Susanna listened with sympathetic interest, trying to picture the girl from Beverly Hills. *Sounds like a Tiffany type to me,* she decided. She didn't share this thought with Anders, though. He'd been in love with Jennifer—maybe he still was.

"I can see why you're not into dating right now," Susanna commiserated. "It takes a long time to get over being hurt like that."

"I'm not only thinking about my own feelings," Anders said. His eyes flickered briefly to Susanna's. "I don't want to leave someone the way Jennifer left me."

Susanna nodded, her throat suddenly tight. *He's right. That's the worst thing: being left behind by someone you love.*

In silent accord, they stood up and headed back down the beach. Timber trotted ahead of them, his coat matted with sand and seaweed. "So, that is why it is awkward," Anders concluded. "But pretty soon the girls will figure out how boring I am."

Susanna laughed. "Don't count on it. First of all, you're not boring. And if anything, from Tiffany and Company's point of view, playing hard to get only makes you more of a challenge."

"Same for you, eh? With the guys."

"It *has* been kind of weird lately." She stuck her hands in the kangaroo pocket of her navy blue Cal Berkeley sweatshirt. "It's like, people gave me a while to mourn Seth, but then right after New Year's, bang. The phone started ringing. Senior prom's still months off, but I've already had three guys ask me to go!" She shook her head. "I don't know, maybe it's my own fault for sending out signals that everything's fine with me and I'm ready to get back into the scene."

"But you do not want to go out with these guys?"

"I don't care about the prom," Susanna declared. "I don't want to date. I don't want to be in a relationship. Not for a long time anyway."

Anders snapped his fingers in mock disappointment. "And I was just about to ask you for a date," he joked.

She gave him a playful shove. "Watch it, buddy."

"It is funny, isn't it?" he said.

"What?"

"Us."

She laughed. "Yeah. Carly would croak if she knew I'd just told you—Anders Lund, the guy the other girls at A.H.S. are all fighting over—on no account, ever, to even *think* about asking me out."

"We are a good pair, then," Anders observed. "You are safe with me."

"Ditto," she promised cheerfully.

"So, I want all the juicy details. *All,*" Carly repeated, her tone breathlessly expectant, as she drove Susanna to school on Monday morning. "What's going on with you and Anders?"

"Me and who?" asked Susanna, deadpan.

Carly shifted the old V.W. Beetle's gears, then gave Susanna's arm a pinch. "I called you, like, *twenty* times this past weekend, and every time, your mom or dad said, 'She's mountain biking with Anders.' 'She and Anders went whale watching.' And last week, you guys did something together practically every single day after school! So . . . ?"

"So?" Susanna echoed.

Carly groaned, exasperated. "Look, Reyes. I'm not jealous, if that's what you're worried about. I think it's great that you're the one who snagged Anders. You absolutely deserve the very best. So?" she repeated impatiently. "I'm waiting!"

Susanna laughed. "We're just friends, Carly. We really *did* go biking and whale watching."

"I suppose even whale watching could be romantic with Anders," Carly mused.

"It wasn't romantic," Susanna swore. "Seriously. It's strictly platonic."

"Yeah, right."

"Read my lips. *Just friends.*"

"I know you don't like to be gossiped about," said Carly, "but it's too late. Everyone's already buzzing."

"They can buzz all they like." Susanna adjusted her sunglasses and gazed calmly out the car window. "That doesn't change the facts."

"Well, the two of you look pretty cozy, kiddo," Carly persisted.

Susanna switched from defense to offense. "What about you and Brad Westerberg?" she countered. "I saw you looking cozy in the library stacks Friday afternoon."

"We were both looking for books, and they just happened to be on the same shelf," Carly explained, all innocence.

"Blame it on the Dewey decimal system, huh?" teased Susanna.

"We're just friends," Carly said. "Can I help it if we keep bumping into each other?"

"Like at the movies the other night?"

Bright spots of pink colored Carly's cheeks. "What are you talking about?"

"Kate and Jin spotted you two on the way out. And it was the *late* show!"

"Must've been someone else."

"Driving a powder blue V.W. bug? Uh-huh."

Carly turned up the volume on the radio. "Ooh," she said. "I love this new Cranberries song, don't you?"

"You can run but you can't hide, Donovan," Susanna yelled over the music.

Carly cupped a hand to her ear. "What? Can't hear you!"

They drove the rest of the way to A.H.S. with the radio blasting. It was tempting to keep giving Carly a hard time, but Susanna decided to let her off the hook for the moment. *I'll bug her more later,* she thought, smiling to herself. *Just like I'm sure she'll bug me about my new "boyfriend" Anders!*

"So, I'm split down the middle," Susanna told Anders as she squeezed a packet of dressing on her chef's salad. They'd bumped into each other on the way into the cafeteria and had grabbed a corner table. Then, as usual, they'd plunged deep into an animated conversation. "I used to be really set on doing the pre-med thing in college," Susanna went on. "Maybe go into research. But lately, I've felt more like taking a nontraditional route, majoring in art or something. I mean, I just don't know if I have what it takes to be a doctor. I don't know if I can deal with that kind of intensity, day in and day out."

Anders munched his sandwich, considering. "But this is okay. You do not have to make up your mind yet, right? You can go to college and take lots of different courses and see what feels right. You can take science and art. In Norway, if you want to go into medicine, you have to choose your career early. After high school, you go straight into a combined college and medical school program. It is better, the way they do it here."

"Wow," said Susanna. "Yeah, you're right. There's no way I'd know, if you asked me on graduation day, what I really want to do with my life. Wow," she repeated. Then she grinned at Anders. "Hey, did you hear yourself just now? That was maybe five or six complex sentences in pretty much perfect English. You're really making progress!"

"Thanks," he said, looking shyly pleased.

They ate for a minute in silence. Then Anders tipped his head, smiling at her quizzically. "Susanna, I just noticed something."

"What?"

He looked around, then lowered his voice. "I'm eating my sandwich."

Susanna's eyebrows furrowed. "And that's noteworthy for what reason?"

"Usually, I don't get a chance to eat during lunch period," he said. "I'm too busy talking to Alicia and Tiffany and the others."

Comprehension dawned. "Oh, I see." Susanna glanced around the cafeteria, curious. She'd been so into her conversation with Anders that she hadn't noticed that no one had come over to sit with them. Instead of the usual stampede, even die-hard Anders fans like Shannon and Rachel were keeping their distance. *But we're definitely getting checked out,* Susanna observed.

She leaned forward with her elbows on the table, her eyes sparkling with amusement. "I think I know what's going on. Everybody thinks we're the latest hot new romance at A.H.S."

"Sorry," Anders said, bemused. "I hope it does not embarrass you."

"Not at all," she assured him. "It *is* kind of nice to eat lunch in peace."

Anders finished his sandwich and began munching grapes, his expression thoughtful. "It is too bad that soon people will figure out that you're not my girlfriend," he said.

Susanna tilted her head to one side. "How come?"

"Well, if I really *did* have a girlfriend, the other girls would leave me alone for good."

"But the point is I'm not your—" Suddenly, she caught on to his train of thought. "*Oh.* You mean we could . . . ?"

"It would benefit you too," Anders pointed out. "You wouldn't have to keep turning down prom date invitations."

Susanna laughed. "You're not serious, are you?"

Anders shrugged, smiling sheepishly. "Why not? As you say in America, what do we have to lose?"

Susanna considered the startling proposition. Pretending to be boyfriend and girlfriend! Anders was right: It made sense in a strange way. It might even work. She imagined saying the words out loud, casually to her friends and acquaintances. "Yeah, I'm going out with Anders Lund now. . . ." She felt a pang. *I can't do that to Seth,* she thought. *Not if I want to stay loyal to his memory, and I do.* "I don't know, Anders," she said.

"No, sure," he responded. "It was just a silly idea."

"Well, not necessarily." Now she found herself arguing the other side. "You're probably right. It makes sense in a strange way. It might even work!"

"Should we try it, then?"

Susanna bit her lip, thinking. *I couldn't pull it off. But it would be such a relief. . . .* "Yes, let's try it," she told Anders. "But are you sure you're up to the challenge? All this deception, an honest guy like you?"

He smiled, his sea blue eyes crinkling. "Sure. It could not be more difficult than carrying your friend Carly on cross-country skis for two miles."

Susanna laughed. "That's right, you're Superman. I forgot! Okay." She drew in a deep breath, fixing her resolution. *It's for the best,* she told herself. "People think we're dating, so we'll pretend we *are* dating," she declared.

SEVEN

"I KNEW IT!" Carly shrieked triumphantly. "I knew, I knew, I *knew* you two were getting it on!"

Susanna, Carly, Jin, and Kate were wedged into a back booth at the Altavista Grill after school, sharing a large basket of onion rings and a pitcher of diet soda. At Carly's outburst, Susanna didn't have to fake a blush—her face turned red for real. "Geez, relax already. I didn't say we were 'getting it on.' We're still getting to know each other. Taking it slow."

"You should have heard her the other day," Carly said to Kate and Jin. "She was *so* full of it. 'We're just friends.'"

"It was true," Susanna protested. "It started out that way, I swear."

"So, what happened?" Jin wanted to know.

Susanna had forgotten that, naturally, her friends would demand all the gory details. *Anders and I*

76

better compare notes later, she thought. *Get our stories straight.* "Well," she began, sipping her soda to buy some time. "Like I said, we *were* just friends at first. He found me when I was lost in the state park that day, remember? That was the first time we really talked. The next day I took him mountain biking, and we just started to do stuff together. And then . . ." The three girls waited breathlessly. Susanna shrugged. "*You* know," she finished lamely.

"No, we don't," said Jin as she speared an onion ring with her fork. "Elaborate, please."

"Where, when, and how?" Kate prodded.

"I guess we were . . . in the car," Susanna ad-libbed. "It was Monday—no, Tuesday—night. We went out for ice cream, and on the way home—"

"His driveway or yours?" Carly cut in.

Susanna blinked. "Um . . . uh . . . mine. I think."

"You don't sound too sure of yourself," Jin noted, laughing. "I'd have thought a first smooch with Anders would be more memorable!"

Susanna blushed. "It was. It's just that—"

"It's just that she was totally blown away by it," Carly supplied. "Of course she can't think straight!"

"Yeah. That's it," Susanna said.

"So, who made the first move?" Kate wanted to know.

Susanna considered for a moment, picturing the imaginary seduction scene. Anders was so polite. . . . "I did," she concluded.

Carly grinned. "Ha. And you were the one a

few weeks ago claiming you weren't in the least interested in even meeting Anders!"

"Silly me," Susanna said with a smile.

Kate reached across the table to squeeze Susanna's hand. "I'm really happy for you, Suze. I know it's been hard, you know, since . . . I'm really happy," she repeated.

"Me too," Jin concurred.

"Me three," said Carly.

"Thanks," Susanna said. She was touched by their sincerity—it almost made her feel guilty for telling such a whopping lie. Almost, but not quite. Word would get out fast now. *I'm Anders's girlfriend,* she thought, *which means I don't have to be anyone else's girlfriend. Which means I can just be myself.*

"Why aren't you sitting with Anders?" Kate wanted to know the next day at morning assembly.

Susanna had been about to flop into a seat next to Kate and Carly in the back of the auditorium. At Kate's question, she caught herself. "I'm going to. I was just saying hi. Have you seen him?"

"Five rows forward, four seats to the right," Carly replied.

"Thanks, Official Eyes and Ears of A.H.S.," Susanna said. "Well, later."

She walked forward a few rows, then scrambled over half a dozen pairs of legs to get to the seat next to Anders, feeling extremely self-conscious. "Hi," she said to him, scrunching down into the chair with her knees propped against the seat in front of her.

"Hi," he replied.

"So, Anders." She lowered her voice. "How's it going?"

Anders looked around, then turned back to her. "Tiffany and Rachel were just on their way over here. Thanks to you, I'm safe," he reported. "How about you?"

Curtis and Austin had both been hovering as she entered the auditorium, but now Susanna noticed they'd both retreated. "Yeah, I'm glad we have each other," she agreed. "I mean, we don't really *have* each other, but we 'have' each other. You know what I mean!"

He chuckled. "I know what you mean."

"Before you get too comfortable, though, you should know that this pretending to be going out thing is going to take a little more work than we anticipated. We have to hang out together a lot more."

"How much?" he asked.

She thought back to when she and Seth had first fallen in love, trying to be analytical about memories that made her heart ache. She and Seth had been totally attached at the hip, making out whenever they got a chance and hardly ever coming up for air. "Pretty much all the time." She made a list for Anders, ticking each item off on her fingers. "We have to meet at our lockers before school, eat lunch together, sit with each other in study hall, hang out after school and on weekends . . ."

"Wow." He raised his eyebrows. "You weren't kidding when you said all the time!"

"Well, that's how real couples act," she pointed out. "Real couples at A.H.S. anyhow. Is it different in Norway?"

He shook his head. "No, it is the same."

The high-school principal stepped up to the podium and began making announcements. Susanna continued in a whisper. "I hope it's not too much of a chore."

Anders gave her one of his slow half smiles. "It will be okay. I kind of like you."

She socked his arm. "I kind of like you too."

"I forgot to tell you about the most important part of being boyfriend and girlfriend," Susanna called over her shoulder to Anders a few days later.

They'd driven to the Napa Valley with the mountain bikes on the car rack so they could tour the wine country's back roads. "What is that?" Anders wondered.

"Senior prom," she replied.

There wasn't any traffic, so Anders accelerated to ride alongside her. "I thought you said you did not want to go to the prom."

"I didn't," Susanna explained. "But now that we're dating—or pretending to—I have to. I mean, senior prom is the ultimate. Literally. It's the last bash, then you graduate and you're gone. So it's a really, really big deal for everybody in the class, but especially for couples."

"I see." Anders absorbed this information with a serious expression. "So, you and I should go to this prom together?"

"Yeah, I think we have to," Susanna replied. She cast a sideways smile at him. "If we don't break up before then, that is. That's the worst, when a couple breaks up right before the prom. Total crisis."

Anders grinned. "Okay. Let's agree not to break up before the prom."

They pedaled another mile, then stopped their bikes at the entrance to a small, out-of-the-way winery. "I love it here this time of year," Susanna said, gesturing to a meadow full of bright yellow blossoms.

"What is the name of that flower?" Anders asked her.

"Mustard grass. It's just a weed," she told him. "But it's pretty, isn't it?"

Anders nodded. "Yes," he agreed. He was looking at Susanna, though, not the mustard grass. She'd taken off her bike helmet so the breeze could blow through her long hair. Her face was glowing from sunshine and exercise, her golden-brown eyes sparkling like amber jewels.

I can't believe I ever thought she was like Jennifer, Anders reflected, recalling his first impression of her. The two girls couldn't be less alike. True, they were both beautiful, but Jennifer's beauty seemed common compared to Susanna's. As for Jennifer's personality, now that he wasn't blinded by infatuation, Anders realized that she had been a little bit shallow. One thing was for sure: He hadn't been able to talk to her the way he talked to Susanna. Jennifer wasn't interested in serious things, she just wanted to have a good time. *She didn't care that much about me,* he concluded silently, *or she wouldn't have treated me the way she did.*

Anders snapped out of his reverie. *What am I doing, comparing Susanna and Jennifer? Susanna's not really my girlfriend; it's not the same thing at all.*

"Are you getting tired of this?" he asked out loud.

Susanna shook her head. "I never get tired of biking around here, especially in the spring, when all the wildflowers are blooming."

"No, I meant . . . this." He pointed to himself, smiling crookedly. "Me. This pretending."

She flipped her hair back before putting her helmet back on. "No way. I'm having fun. And besides, it's working. Your life is less complicated, isn't it?"

"Yes," Anders said as he mounted his bike. But inside, he wasn't sure. *She's not really your girlfriend,* he reminded himself again as he pedaled after Susanna.

"So, Suze, now that the movie's over . . ." Carly grabbed a handful of microwave popcorn and stuffed it into her mouth. When she was done chewing, she continued, "I want to know what it's like to kiss Anders."

It was Friday night, and Carly had come over to Susanna's house to watch a video. Susanna was "free" because the Collinas had taken Anders into the city to hear the symphony. Now Susanna hit the rewind button on the remote control. "Geez, could you get a little more personal, Donovan?"

"So shoot me, I'm curious. I just wondered if maybe he did it differently. Like, some special Norwegian way."

Susanna giggled. "You have the *strangest* mind, Donovan."

"Well, so does he?"

"The strangest *one-track* mind," Susanna amended.

Carly grinned. "Okay, I'm obsessed with sex, we've established that. Back to kissing Anders. You do kiss, don't you?"

"Of course! All the time."

"So, is it great or just so-so?"

Susanna closed her eyes for a moment, praying that she wouldn't have to describe her and Anders's fake make-out sessions in too much detail. "It's great," Susanna told Carly. "He's a great kisser. I'm sorry to say, though, that Norwegians do it the same as Americans."

"Is he the snuggly teddy-bear type, or is he more, like, intense and romantic?"

"Um . . . a little of both."

"Can't keep his hands off you, huh?"

Susanna flushed. "Uh, no."

"It's funny, because in public you two are pretty mellow," Carly commented. "I don't even think I've seen you holding hands."

"Really?" Susanna made a mental note that she and Anders should experiment with some minor P.D.A. in the hall at school, for the sake of the charade. "Well, Anders is kind of shy. He doesn't like drawing attention to himself."

"He doesn't have to *draw* it," Carly said. "It's already there." She grabbed the remote from Susanna and pointed it at the television screen. "Late show time. Leno or Letterman?"

They polished off the popcorn and watched TV.

Susanna sank into the sofa cushions, relieved that Carly was through—at least momentarily—with her sex-life inquisition. The conversation had left Susanna feeling squirmy and uncomfortable. For some reason, now she couldn't stop thinking about kissing Anders . . . and wondering why she was able to imagine it so vividly.

"You want to hold hands," Anders stated.

Susanna felt her face turn as red as a chili pepper. "Just so no one suspects," she said quickly. "Carly was noticing that you and I don't *act* like a couple in front of other people. But if you don't want to . . . I mean, if kids in Norway don't . . ."

"No, no." All of a sudden, Anders's face was looking a little sunburned too. "It's a good idea. We hold hands in Norway, of course. Yes. Sure. Great."

"So," said Susanna. They stood for a few seconds in front of Anders's locker, shyly avoiding each other's eyes. "Um . . . I guess I need to stop by my locker before homeroom."

"I'll walk you there," he offered.

Susanna held out her hand, and Anders awkwardly took it. All at once, she felt a surge of unexpected emotions. She hadn't held hands with a boy since Seth; she hadn't realized how much she missed the sweet, companionable feeling. *It's not just the feeling I miss,* she reminded herself, *it's the person.* When Seth used to take her hand, it always felt natural and comfortable and exciting at the same time. They were so in tune, it was almost as if they weren't two separate bodies.

She and Anders started to walk, but for some reason, it didn't feel right. "Wait a minute. Let's try it this way," Susanna whispered, hoping nobody was watching this trial run. Releasing his hand, she turned her wrist the other way, then twined her fingers through his. "How's that? Better?"

"It is very nice," he told her.

They walked down the corridor, awkwardly trying to match their strides. Susanna and Seth had been about the same height, but Susanna practically had to jog to keep up with Anders, whose legs were about twice as long as hers. The hallway was crowded and they kept getting jostled. Susanna's shoulder bumped against Anders's arm and she stepped on his foot. "Sorry," she mumbled.

He gripped her hand a little more tightly. "No sweat."

"No sweat?" She laughed up at him. "Where'd you get that one?"

"TV," he told her, smiling. "Why? Didn't I say it right?"

"Yeah, you said it right, but you must've been watching old seventies' reruns," she replied, laughing again. "'No sweat.'"

They reached her locker. Anders was still holding tight to her fingers. "Um, you'll have to let go so I can dial my combination," she told him.

"Oh, right." He dropped her hand fast. "Sorry."

Susanna rummaged around for the books she needed for her first couple of classes, sticking them into her shoulder bag. Then she slammed the locker shut. "Ready to roll," she reported.

This time, Anders took her hand in an easy, natural fashion. He swung it lightly as they walked. At one point, ushering her into a stairwell, he touched her briefly at the waist. "We're getting the hang of this, don't you think?" he asked.

"I bet we look pretty convincing," Susanna agreed.

They continued toward her homeroom, saying hello to people as they went. Susanna could see that everyone was registering the hand-holding business, taking mental note: "Yep, they're a couple. It's official."

It was gratifying, but for some reason, it was also disturbing. Susanna was happy to say goodbye to Anders at the door to her homeroom. Yeah, they were getting the hang of it. Holding hands was good strategy. But Susanna hadn't counted on one thing. Easing into a seat in the back row of Ms. Broyard's homeroom, she fanned herself with a spiral notebook. A feeling of guilt washed over her; her cheeks were pink and hot. *It didn't mean anything,* she reminded herself. *It was just a pose.* It didn't mean she'd betrayed Seth's memory.

But the fact of the matter was, holding hands with Anders had caused her body temperature to rise about twenty degrees. No, Susanna hadn't counted on that.

EIGHT

Susanna and Anders had made a date to go to a party at Alicia Van Etten's house that night. For once, they were both looking forward to a party, knowing they'd actually be able to enjoy themselves. There'd be no predatory girls circling Anders, no boys trailing Susanna around with wistful, puppy-dog eyes. When Susanna suggested they just meet at Alicia's, though, Anders shook his head firmly. "It would not look like boyfriend and girlfriend," he pointed out. "Mrs. Collina will let me borrow her car. I will pick you up at eight-thirty. Okay?"

Now it was 8:20 P.M., and she was in her bedroom experiencing what she and her friends always referred to as a "clothing crisis." Susanna hadn't had one in ages, not since her first few dates with Seth, but this was the real thing, a full-fledged C.C., as in standing in front of her closet in her underwear in the depths of despair because through some quirk in the space-time continuum, though she had dozens of outfits, she had absolutely *nothing* to wear.

Susanna flung a handful of tops and skirts onto her bed. Black: too somber. White: too daytime. She shrugged into a red dress, took a quick look in her full-length mirror, then shrugged back out of it. "I could always wear jeans," she muttered to herself, but she didn't want to wear jeans. In the first place, Alicia lived in the biggest, fanciest house in Altavista; and it was Alicia's eighteenth birthday, so she herself would probably be decked out in something dressy from a chic San Francisco boutique. That in itself wasn't reason enough not to go casual, though. There'd be plenty of denim and flannel at the party. No, as she stared at herself in the mirror, Susanna had to admit that she wasn't dressing to impress Alicia. She was primping because she was going to the party with Anders.

"I've got a new boyfriend, theoretically," Susanna rationalized. "I have to look nice. People would think it was weird if I showed up totally slouchy. I have to wear the kind of outfit that'll knock Anders's socks off. Theoretically."

It was past eight-thirty when she finally decided on a pair of loose, cinnamon-colored, raw silk trousers and a black, cream, and cinnamon striped vest that left her arms bare. As she brushed her hair and slipped on a pair of silver and onyx earrings, she could hear Anders down the hall in the living room talking to her parents. "Makeup, yes or no?" she asked herself; deciding yes, lipstick and mascara were in order. Perfume too. But she didn't need any other cosmetics. There was plenty of color in her cheeks—almost too much—and her eyes couldn't have been brighter.

As she stuffed some odds and ends into a small black leather purse and put on black flats, Susanna breathed deeply to see whether she could slow her pulse. *I'm nervous,* she thought, fanning her face with her pocketbook. *This is crazy.*

She started down the hall to where Anders was waiting for her. *I know, it's because it's our first party together. We'll be under a lot of scrutiny.* Yes, that was it, Susanna decided, relieved. Her heart was fluttery at the prospect of having to fake out all her friends. *Phew.* For a minute there, she'd really been worried. But of course she didn't have a crush on Anders. It didn't matter to her in the least whether he thought she looked pretty. That was the whole point of their nonrelationship. Their passion for each other was pure playacting.

But Susanna's pulse kept jumping, and it gave an especially lively skip when she came around a bend in the hall and saw Anders standing in profile, wavy brown locks sweeping back from his forehead, the strong line of his jaw, his sunburnt cheekbones. And when he turned and looked at her and his blue eyes lit up with admiration and he smiled that slow, shy smile . . .

Playacting, Susanna reminded herself.

The first floor of the sprawling Van Etten residence was packed with teenagers. Susanna and Anders bumped into Carly by the dining room buffet. "Did you and Brad have a fight?" Susanna asked Carly.

"No, we didn't have a fight," Carly replied, examining a platter of crudités before choosing a carrot stick.

"But you're avoiding him," Susanna observed, extremely conscious of the fact that Anders was holding her hand in casual, devoted-couple fashion.

"We're not going out," Carly reminded Susanna briskly. She snapped the carrot stick in two with unnecessary vigor. "So it's technically not a question of avoiding him. I'm interested in talking to other people tonight, that's all."

"Well, he looks really sad," said Susanna.

"He does," Anders agreed.

Carly shrugged. "It can't have anything to do with me. By the way, Suze, did you see who's home for the weekend?"

"Colin Van Etten?" Susanna guessed.

"I had a *huge* crush on Alicia's big brother back when I was a freshman and he was a senior," Carly recounted for Anders's benefit. "He's even more gorgeous now, don't you think, Suze?"

Susanna didn't have an opinion. "He goes to San Francisco State, right?"

Carly nodded. "And I applied there, so we were just talking about it. I think I'll head back that way. In case a slow song comes on," she added meaningfully.

Susanna watched Carly weave her way purposefully toward Colin Van Etten. Someone else was watching too. In addition to rumpled khakis and a black Polo shirt, Brad Westerberg wore a crestfallen expression that made him look even younger than he actually was. "Poor guy," Susanna said to Anders. "He really likes her. And she likes him too, but she just won't admit it."

"Complicated," Anders observed.

"Yep." Susanna shot a glance at him out of the corner of her eye. He looked completely relaxed and unflappable. *He's not having any weird feelings,* Susanna thought. Testing him a little, she asked, "Aren't you glad *we* don't have to worry about any of that romance stuff?"

He didn't have to think long. "Yes," he said with certainty, "but we still need to make the right appearance. Perhaps we should dance."

"Sure."

They joined the frenzy of bodies in the Van Etten living room, where the large-screen television was tuned to a music video station, the stereo speakers blasting. The song was fast, but Susanna and Anders had to dance pretty close because of the crowd. Still, it wasn't as nerve-racking as holding hands. They weren't actually in physical contact. And Anders was entertaining when he danced, really into the music and not at all concerned with how he looked, the way American guys usually were. Susanna couldn't help smiling.

Then the video ended and a new song came on. A slow song. Susanna stopped, her feet rooted to the parquet floor.

Anders hesitated too. "Uh, do you— should we . . . ?"

"We could take a break and get something to drink," Susanna said. But moments like this were the ones couples waited for. All around them, boys and girls were blissfully wrapping their arms around each other. Susanna saw Alicia, Shannon, and Tiffany watching her and Anders, their expressions nakedly envious. "No, we'd better keep dancing." -

Anders stepped toward her. He put his arms around her waist, and she slipped hers around his neck. "Is this right?" he murmured, his lips close to her hair. "Do you think this looks like slow dancing for real?"

Susanna's body tingled all over. It sure *felt* like slow dancing for real. "Yes," she whispered.

They swayed to the music, moving as one. Susanna was intensely aware of the whole length of Anders's body touching hers: thighs, hips, chest. She hadn't been this close to a boy since Seth, and for the first minute or two, she was almost unbearably tense. Then, gradually, she relaxed. Her body molded into the curve of Anders's arms—they fit together like pieces of a puzzle. Instead of embarrassment, she felt herself suffused with a vibrantly warm sense of pleasure.

Risking a glance up at him, Susanna caught Anders looking down at her, an unguarded expression on his face. When their eyes met, he flushed. "I hope you are not minding this too much," he said gruffly.

Susanna ducked her head, hiding her face against his chest. She wasn't sure what kind of unintentional message her own eyes might be sending. "Um, no," she replied. "It's okay."

It was way more than okay, but she wasn't about to admit it. She was too confused by her feelings . . . or, rather, by the fact that she even *had* feelings. What was happening to her?

"I had a really good time tonight," Anders said to Susanna as he drove her home from Alicia's party.

"Me too." Susanna pointed to the illuminated clock on the dashboard that read 1:00 A.M. "I can't believe we stayed so late. Are you going to get in trouble with Mr. and Mrs. C.?"

"No. My curfew is two o'clock," Anders answered. "They are very . . . liberated?"

Susanna laughed. "You mean, liberal."

Anders glanced at her. In the shadowy car, her face looked pale and soft against her slightly tousled hair. He realized that he didn't want to say goodnight quite yet. "We could stay out a little longer," he suggested. "A bunch of people were going to hang out at Shady Glen. Jason and others."

"I know," said Susanna. The wooded town park was a popular destination for romance-minded couples and teens with six-packs. "But to be honest, the underage drinking thing isn't really my cup of tea. Or should I say, can of beer?"

"I understand what you are saying," Anders assured her. "There is a lot of drinking for teenagers in Norway, but I am not very much under it."

"Into it," Susanna corrected with a smile.

He smiled back at her. "Right."

He drove on to her house. Pulling into the

driveway, he turned off the headlights and the engine, leaving the key in the ignition so that they could listen to the radio. "Will you get in trouble for being late?" he asked.

"No, I don't have any curfew at all," she replied. "My parents are *really* liberated."

For a minute, they sat in the darkness, the music pulsing around them. Anders was playing a rock tape he'd brought with him from Norway. "Do you like this song?" he asked.

She shifted in her bucket seat, facing him. "Yes, but I'd like it better if I knew what they were saying."

He hummed along for a line, then translated for her. "I want you to stay with me tonight."

"Oh," Susanna said, her eyes sliding shyly away from his.

She looked straight ahead through the dark windshield, but she hadn't completely cut herself off. Her body was still angled toward his. Without thinking, Anders placed a hand on her shoulder. Her jacket lay across her lap, and the skin of her bare shoulder was warm under his fingertips. "Susanna," he said softly.

She looked at him, her eyes large and meltingly dark, a stray strand of hair tangled in her long lashes. As he looked into her face, he felt himself grow breathless, as if he'd just jogged up a steep hillside with a heavy pack. He had never seen anyone so beautiful—not any of the girls he knew in Bergen. Not even Jennifer. He repeated her name in a whisper. "Susanna."

She parted her lips as if to reply but didn't speak. Her eyes were wide with surprise and a vulnerability he'd never seen there before. He expected her to turn away, but she didn't.

Feelings rose up in him, feelings he didn't know how to put into words, English or Norwegian. Instead of saying anything, Anders bent his head to Susanna's. She started to meet him halfway, lifting her mouth to his. Their faces were only inches apart. At the last second, she pulled back abruptly. "What are we *doing?*" She giggled nervously. "No one's watching. We can drop the act."

Anders's hand was still on her shoulder. He yanked it back quickly. "Of course," he murmured. "Sorry. I did not mean—"

Susanna recovered her composure fast. "It's all right," she said, her breezy tone turning the awkward moment into a joke. Her dark eyes had become opaque, unreadable. "Hey, it's like method acting. We were just getting into our parts."

Anders nodded silently, not knowing how else to respond.

She hopped out of the car before he could get out and walk around to open her door. "Good night," she said, slamming the door shut.

"See you," he said, echoing her casual tone.

Susanna slipped into the darkness, a shadow hastening toward the house.

When she'd disappeared, Anders restarted the car. His tone had been neutral, but his emotions were anything but. *I almost kissed her. I wanted to kiss her,* he realized.

He put a hand to his head. The blood was pounding in his temples. "Stop thinking about it," he advised himself sternly as he steered the Subaru along the dark, winding road. But it was easier said than done. Susanna's perfume lingered in the car. He could still feel the silk of her skin under his hand, sense her warmth as she leaned close to him. How could he stop wondering what it would be like to hold her in his arms when all at once it was what he wanted more than anything in the world?

He couldn't give in to these crazy feelings. *After all, I'm Norwegian, not American,* Anders reminded himself. *I don't need an American girlfriend.* As for getting a crush on Susanna Reyes, it was exactly the kind of thing he'd been trying to avoid back when he proposed that they pretend to be dating. "I will not fall in love with another American girl," Anders declared as he shifted gears and stepped on the gas pedal. Particularly not *this* American girl.

Susanna stood just inside the house, leaning back against the door. Adrenaline flooded her veins, and her heart thumped as if she'd just narrowly escaped some grave danger. And in a way, maybe she had. She and Anders had almost ended their fake date with a not-so-fake goodnight kiss.

Susanna hugged herself, her whole body trembling. Why had she let her guard down? When Anders touched her shoulder, she knew it was time to get away, to put some distance between them. Instead, his hand on her skin was like a match striking. She'd been flooded with a sudden blazing warmth, and when he'd moved toward her, she'd responded instinctively. They'd come so close. . . .

She tried to laugh it off, as she had in the car for his benefit. "Hormones," she muttered as she kicked off her shoes and padded barefoot down the hall to her bedroom. Hard to believe sensible people like her and Anders could be so impressionable. A little moonlight and music and look at them!

It was funny, but at the same time, it was not so funny. Because her heart was still slamming against her rib cage, and she couldn't prevent her slightly dizzy thoughts from taking her to a forbidden place. What if she *hadn't* drawn away? What if his hand had slid from her shoulder to the back of her neck? What if his lips had brushed hers?

In her room, Susanna turned on a light, attempting to banish these unbidden images. Standing in front of the mirror as she had while dressing before her date with Anders, she looked searchingly at her own face. Her complexion was flushed, her eyes a little wild. *I look as if I did kiss him,* Susanna thought, turning even redder.

Nearly every girl in Altavista had fallen head over heels for shy, handsome Anders Lund from Bergen, Norway. Why should she be any different? *Because I have to be,* Susanna reflected. *I am different.* She wanted to believe that that was still true, that she alone was impervious to Anders's charms. But after what had taken place in the car just now . . .

Susanna switched off the light, but she continued to frown anxiously at the darkened mirror. The whole point of the boyfriend/girlfriend ruse was to protect herself from falling in love. Was the plan backfiring?

NINE

By the bright, clear light of a sunny spring morning, Susanna found herself seeing things differently. As she drove to school on Monday, she kept picturing herself and Anders in the car Friday night, zeroing in for a kiss and then springing apart as if they'd been jabbed with red-hot branding irons. The more she replayed the scene in her mind, the more comic it became. It was too bad Carly, Kate, and Jin didn't know the truth about her relationship with Anders—she hated to waste a good story!

She came up behind Anders at his locker and tapped him on the shoulder. He jumped. "Oh, *hallo*."

"How'd you sleep this weekend?" she asked cheerfully.

"Um, fine," he said, clearly startled by the question.

"You mean you didn't have nightmares about me morphing into Tiffany Stone and trying to jump you?" she teased.

"Er," said Anders, "excuse me?"

"The other night. Us. In the car. Were we ridiculous or what?"

"Uh—"

"I just want you to know, Anders, that you're safe with me," Susanna babbled on. "Absolutely. One hundred percent. It was just a fluke."

He wrinkled his forehead. "A fluke?"

"A goof, a blooper," she translated unhelpfully. "I think we should make sure we don't have a language barrier here, though—that we're both clear on where we stand."

"We are standing in the hallway of the high school," Anders said.

"No, silly." Susanna laughed. "Figuratively speaking. Where we stand in relation to each other. What we mean to each other, *really*. We're friends just *pretending* to be more than friends, right?"

Before, he'd seemed confused, but now she could tell he knew exactly what she was getting at. "Friends pretending to be more than friends," he repeated.

"It's a game."

"A game."

"If . . . if that's how you want it to be," Susanna added, all at once sounding a little less certain.

There was a long, emotionally charged pause. Susanna held her breath, half hoping that Anders would challenge her. His expression was unreadable as he answered slowly, choosing his words with care. "I think that is how it should be," he agreed.

"Great," said Susanna, swallowing her

disappointment. "Well . . . I need to run over to the library before homeroom." She rose on her toes to give his cheek a fast, impersonal peck for appearance's sake. "So long."

"So long," he echoed.

As she hurried off, her own words seemed to trail her down the corridor, mocking her. *"It's a game . . . friends just pretending to be more than friends. . . ." Maybe if we say it often enough, it will be true,* she thought.

A week later, as far as Susanna could tell, she and Anders had reached an unspoken agreement that their best bet was to play it safe, spending time together out-of-doors and preferably by daylight, avoiding late-night drives and other potentially romantic scenarios. Her softball team had begun its season, and Anders dutifully showed up to watch practices as well as games. They went together to a party at Carly's house, and afterward, Anders dropped her off at the bottom of the driveway. Things were pretty much back to normal.

On this particular Sunday afternoon, they'd decided to go on a hike. Susanna was in a good mood, at ease with Anders and with herself for the first time since the almost-kiss. She really did enjoy his company more than anyone else's; it would have been a shame to sacrifice a perfectly satisfying friendship.

"Do you remember the first time we hiked here together?" Anders asked as they headed into the state park near her house.

Susanna laughed as she crouched to retie one of

her bootlaces. "Yeah, I remember. You had to help me find my way out of a park I'm supposed to know as well as my own backyard."

"You weren't really lost," Anders allowed. "You just thought you were."

"Well, notice I left Timber at home today," Susanna said. "I'm not taking any chances!"

They took the Wildcat Canyon Trail to the top of the ridge. Winter, the rainy season in northern California, had come and gone, leaving the Marin hills lushly green. On either side of the trail, the meadows were a vibrant tapestry of color ranging from bright orange poppies to deep blue lupine. Susanna inhaled the glorious scent of grass and flowers. "It's like paradise, isn't it? Everything's blooming. In a few months, though, the hills will be totally golden and dry. It's beautiful like that too, in a different way. But you won't be here to see it," she added matter-of-factly.

Anders glanced at her. "No."

It was just one word, but something in his tone made Susanna suspect he planned to say more. Avoiding his gaze, she resumed marching along at a brisk pace. "It's getting pretty cloudy," she said, taking refuge in the safe topic of weather. "Think it'll rain?"

Her answer came a few minutes later. The sky, overcast when they began their hike, darkened to charcoal. Gusts of wind whipped Susanna's hair, and raindrops pelted her bare arms and legs.

She and Anders stopped to throw on waterproof anoraks. At first, the rain felt refreshing. Soon, though, it became a downpour. "Come on,"

Susanna shouted to Anders, breaking into a jog. "Let's head back down into the trees."

The path forked just a few yards ahead of them. Veering to the right, they sprinted downhill. Soon they were in dense forest, the branches overhead protecting them from the shower. They slowed down, breathless and drenched. "You should see yourself," Susanna gasped, giggling. Anders's hair was dripping as if he'd been standing under a waterfall. A big raindrop hung from the end of his nose. "You look like Timber after a bath."

"Thank you very much," Anders said wryly. "I am too polite, of course, to comment on your appearance."

Just ahead of them, a fallen pine tree leaned at an angle against some other trees, creating a makeshift tent. "Why don't we sit here for a few minutes," he suggested, "and wait out the worst of the storm?"

"What if there's lightning?" Susanna looked anxiously skyward. "It wouldn't be the safest place then."

Anders tipped his head back and breathed deeply. "No," he replied, "I don't smell lightning."

Susanna started giggling again. "You don't *smell* it? Oh, you woodsy Norwegians!"

They crawled under the fallen tree, discovering a bed of relatively dry pine needles. Susanna rubbed her hair and face dry with a sweatshirt she'd pulled from her backpack, then handed it to Anders, who did the same. With his damp hair slicked back, the chiseled planes of his face stood out, making him even more handsome than usual. *Not that I'm noticing,* Susanna thought. Anders's good looks didn't affect her in the least.

She tucked up her knees and hugged them with her arms. Around them, the sound of rain filled the woods. For a few minutes, she and Anders sat quietly, listening. "We were already wet," Susanna remarked after a while. "We might as well have kept on going."

"I like it here," Anders said.

She decided not to admit that she liked it too, being alone with Anders in this little forest hide-away. Alone . . . *Better fill up this silence,* Susanna thought. It probably wasn't a good idea to just sit staring at each other, especially since Anders had taken off his anorak and his wet T-shirt was cling-ing to his torso in a disturbingly attractive fashion.

"So," she said out loud, "I've been helping you with your English all these weeks, but you've hardly taught me any words in Norwegian."

Anders smiled, clearly pleased at her interest. "What would you like to learn?"

"How do you say . . ." She looked up at the fallen pine's branches. "Forest?"

"Skog," Anders supplied.

"Skog," Susanna attempted. She laughed at herself. "I thought that would be an easy one."

"Ask me more," he invited.

"Okay. Hiking."

"Gå på tur."

"Skiing."

"Stå på ski."

"Ice cream."

"Iskrem."

Susanna continued to list words, with Anders

103

providing the Norwegian translation. Then they'd both laugh over her awkward pronunciation. "Languages are funny, aren't they?" she observed after a few minutes. "I mean, the fact that we have such different ways of saying things."

"What is amazing, I think," said Anders, "is that the sounds we make are different, of course, but the ideas are the same. We are all talking about the same things."

"Ice cream is a universal fact of life," she agreed, smiling.

"No, seriously," he said. "Different cultures and landscapes give birth to different vocabularies, I know. But we all have words for the basic human realities. Like *mann* and *kvinne*."

"What's that?" she asked.

"Man and woman."

"Oh." For some reason, Susanna felt herself blush. "Yeah, and, like, every society has words for life and death."

"*Liv og død* in Norwegian," Anders told her. "And there is also *elske og hate*."

"Meaning?"

"Love and hate."

"It's too bad there's such a word as hate, though," said Susanna.

"I agree," said Anders. "I like *elske* much better."

"*Elske,*" Susanna repeated. Now her cheeks were really hot. Luckily, it was dim in the shelter of the tree. "It sounds . . . nice. In Norwegian," she added lamely.

"There are other nice words that go with it." His eyes were fixed intently on her face in a way that forced her to look back at him. "*Tiltrukket:* to be attracted. *Hengiven:* to be devoted."

Susanna gulped. *It's a word game,* she reminded herself. They were just passing time waiting out the rain. "I guess it's useful to know these things," she joked. "In case I ever find myself reading a Norwegian romance novel."

"They are words for life, not books," Anders said soberly. He was still staring at her. "You should know what these things mean, Susanna." He put out a hand, brushing her cheek gently with his fingertips. *"Huden din er så myk."*

His touch sent a jolt of electricity coursing through Susanna's body. "W-What did you say?" she stammered.

"Your skin is so soft."

There was no way he could miss her blush now. "Um, thanks," she squeaked.

"Here's another one you should learn," he said. *"Kan jeg kysse deg?"*

There was a question in his voice. They had been sitting face-to-face, Anders cross-legged. Now he leaned closer to her, one arm sliding behind her back. She didn't ask, but he translated for her anyway, quietly. "May I kiss you?"

Susanna stared into Anders's clear blue eyes, feeling as if she were seeing him for the first time, as if a mask had been removed, and she knew her own face was just as naked and revealing. Though they'd been denying it, something had been growing between them for weeks. They were falling in love.

The discovery both thrilled and terrified her. It was too late to run from it, though. Anders had brought it out into the open. "How do you say . . ."—Susanna's voice dropped to a trembling whisper—". . . yes?"

"Ja," Anders murmured.

They both rose to their knees. Anders pulled her body against his. He'd kissed her before, on the cheek, for show in front of their friends. Now he cupped her face in his hands and put his mouth on hers.

For Susanna, everything in the world but Anders seemed to melt away. She couldn't smell the pine needles, hear the rain, feel the hard earth under her knees. There was only his body, his lips.

For a long, delicious moment, she lost herself in the kiss. It felt so good, she didn't want to question whether it was the right thing to do. But gradually, inevitably, her memories and fears pushed back into her consciousness. *No,* she thought.

Susanna pulled away from Anders, flushed and dismayed. "This wasn't supposed to happen," she declared breathlessly.

"But it did." Anders reached out for her again. "Susanna, I—"

She couldn't let him say it. Naming the feeling would make it real, and she wasn't ready to deal with it. "Don't," she begged. Jumping to her feet, she pushed blindly through the branches and ran off into the wet woods.

By the time Anders shouldered both their back-packs, Susanna had disappeared among the dark, dripping tree trunks. He guessed where she was going, though, and followed the trail leading out of the park.

It was still raining, but he didn't feel the chill and damp. He jogged without effort, light-headed with happiness. He'd been living in California for months, and on the surface, he fit right in—with his host family and at Altavista High. People couldn't have been friendlier. But that didn't change the fact that he was a foreigner, thousands of miles from his real home and family. He was aware of it every time he opened his mouth and had to think hard about what he was saying in order to get the English grammar and vocabulary right.

Now, though, in the instant that he acted on his feelings for Susanna, his life had become fluent again. He hadn't been looking for love—quite the opposite—but it had found him anyway.

He caught up with her in her own front yard. Before she could dash up the porch steps, he grasped her arm. "Susanna, wait." She turned and looked up at him, her face wet with rain and tears. "What's the matter?" he asked.

She shook her head. "I'm sorry, Anders. I shouldn't have—we shouldn't have . . . It was a mistake," she finally choked out.

"What was a mistake?"

"Kissing." She stepped away from him, her shoulders hunched inside her dripping-wet anorak. "We got carried away by the roles we've been playing. I think you should go home and we should just pretend this never—"

"No," he declared. "I'm tired of pretending."

"But, Anders." Her eyes widened. "Don't you remember what brought us together in the first place? Seth. Jennifer."

"I remember, but I've changed since then, and so have you," he said, his voice hoarse with urgency. "I can't hide my feelings any longer, Susanna. I never think about Jennifer anymore. I'm in love with you. In love with you in a way I never was with her."

Susanna stared at him. Anders wondered if she could say the same, if she loved him as much as she'd loved Seth, if she was ready to put the past behind her. Hardly breathing, he waited for her to step toward him or turn away. Whatever her choice, he'd honor it.

Susanna hesitated. They faced each other, close enough to touch but not touching. *"Jeg elsker deg,"* Anders said simply. "I love you. That is all."

Suddenly, Susanna was in his arms again, smiling through her tears. She whispered something— "I love you too"? Anders couldn't tell, and it didn't matter. They'd been holding each other at arm's length for so long, now they couldn't get close enough. They didn't need words, in any language. Their kisses said it all.

TEN

"WAIT A MINUTE, whoa, hold on," Carly commanded, holding up her hand for emphasis. "You're losing me here."

"We kissed," Susanna repeated, her eyes starry. "Me and Anders."

When the two girls bumped into each other at the coffee bar Monday morning before school, Susanna had whisked Carly straight outside to a bench under a redwood tree so that she could confide in semiprivacy what had happened in the rain with Anders the day before.

"What's the big deal?" Carly wanted to know. "You make it sound like you bungee jumped off the Golden Gate Bridge. You've been kissing for ages!"

"No, we haven't. That's what I'm trying to tell you! We weren't kissing before. We were just pretending to kiss."

"Pretending?" Carly's forehead creased in

puzzlement. "But you were madly in love and making out all the time and——"

"We *weren't* madly in love," Susanna cut in. "It was all an act back then. But we *are* in love now." Her face was radiant. "Oh, Carly. It's so incredible!"

Carly put down her coffee cup and folded her arms across her chest. "I am absolutely one hundred percent lost," she announced somewhat crabbily. "You and Anders have been the hottest couple at A.H.S. for *weeks,* but it was an *act?*" Now she looked hurt. "You mean, you've been lying to *everyone,* including *me?*"

"It wasn't a lie," said Susanna, trying to defend herself. "It was more like a . . ."

"A lie," said Carly.

"Anders was tired of girls hanging all over him," Susanna explained. "He got totally burned last year in Bergen by this American exchange student, and so he thought it was better not to get involved with anyone here. And I was tired of guys asking me out when I wasn't ready for another relationship because of Seth. So one day, it just occurred to us that if we pretended to be a couple, people might leave us alone. And they did."

"Unbelievable," Carly said.

"I know," agreed Susanna, smiling into her coffee cup.

"I can't believe you didn't tell me what was really going on." Carly was still miffed. "You could have trusted me—I'd have kept the secret."

"It's not that I didn't trust you," Susanna swore. "I didn't trust myself."

"And you didn't tell Jin or Kate either?"

Susanna shook her head.

"And I'm the first to know?"

Susanna nodded.

Carly appeared somewhat mollified. "Well, in that case . . ."

"Thanks for understanding."

Carly laughed. "I didn't say I understand. I still think it was a bizarre thing to do."

"It made perfect sense at the time," Susanna assured her. "For a while, it really did make my life easier. But now . . ."

"What could be more simple than just plain being crazy about somebody?" Carly wanted to know, retrieving her coffee cup and taking a sip.

Susanna wished she could find a way to describe what utter turmoil her emotions were in. On the one hand, she'd been walking on air since that amazing kiss in the woods, and the even more mind-blowing one in her rainy front yard. On the other hand . . . "I am crazy about him," she admitted. "But the school year's almost over. Another eleven weeks, and we graduate and Anders goes back to Bergen."

Carly shrugged. "So?"

"So I just don't know if I can deal with it." Susanna bit her lip. "This is the first time since . . . since Seth. The first time I've had feelings for someone." She frowned, struggling to express herself. "It's like I've been in hibernation or something, and now I'm awake again, but it's almost *too* intense. I'd been guarding my heart so closely. It's so fragile. Now I've taken off that bulletproof vest, you know?"

"Anders won't hurt you," Carly said quietly.

"Not on purpose." Susanna sighed. "But he can't change the fact that he lives on the other side of the planet."

A mild spring breeze rustled through the redwoods. They sat in silence for a few minutes, sipping their coffee. "I still don't think it should matter," Carly said at last. "If you love each other, you shouldn't get hung up on logistics."

"Logistics." Susanna laughed. "Where'd you get that word, Donovan?"

Carly smiled. "Too many syllables for you, Reyes?"

Just then, the homeroom bell rang. They strolled back to the school building. "If you want my final opinion, Suze," said Carly, tossing her cup into a trash bin, "you should forget about tomorrow and live for today. Go for it with Anders."

Forget about tomorrow and live for today. Susanna smiled wistfully to herself. Carly made it sound so easy. Maybe it *was* that easy. *Go for it with Anders*, she thought. *Maybe that's what I'll do.*

"I had fun tonight," Anders told Susanna.

"Me too," she said.

They'd gone out to dinner and a movie, and now they were sitting in Mrs. Collina's Subaru just as they had a few weeks earlier, the night of Alicia's birthday party. This time, though, instead of in Susanna's driveway, they were parked high up in the Marin headlands overlooking the twinkling lights of the Golden Gate Bridge and San Francisco. Also unlike that other night, Susanna wasn't in any hurry for Anders to take her home.

They unbuckled their seat belts so they could wriggle a little closer to each other. Placing her hands on either side of Anders's face, Susanna drew him to her for a kiss.

It was different from the passionate, unexpected, almost desperate kisses they'd exchanged the other day in the rain. Sweeter, softer, more playful, but just as exciting. Susanna shivered with pleasure.

"Are you cold?" Anders asked. "I can close the car windows."

She shook her head, smiling. "Actually, I'm warm. Aren't you?"

"Very," he agreed, his lips finding hers once more. "What do you say, would this be more comfortable in the backseat?" When Susanna looked surprised, he grinned. "We have backseats in Norway too, you know."

The backseat *was* a little roomier. After a few more kisses, they lay peacefully in each other's arms. Susanna pressed her face against Anders's shirt. "I can hear your heartbeat," she told him.

"Fast or slow?"

"Absurdly slow." She tickled his ribs. "You must be in good shape. Those were my best kisses, and it didn't raise your blood pressure one bit."

Anders chuckled. "Believe me, they had an effect."

Susanna hugged him tightly. "Good."

She continued to listen to the steady, soothing thump of Anders's heart while he stroked her hair. "What are you thinking about?" she asked him after a minute.

"I am thinking that I cannot believe my good luck," he replied. "To be here with you."

"We've been hanging out together for months," she reminded him.

He gave her a squeeze. "Not like this."

"Are you sure you're not having second thoughts? You didn't want a girlfriend."

He dropped a kiss on her forehead. "That was because I didn't realize a girl could be as wonderful as you."

Susanna sat up, pushing her hair back from her face. She'd never asked Anders many questions about Jennifer because she knew it was a painful subject, but now it seemed safe to be curious. "What was Jennifer like?" she asked.

"On the inside or the outside?"

"Both, I guess."

"Well, this is what she looks like." Anders took out his wallet. Removing a slightly crumpled photograph, he handed it to Susanna. She couldn't help feeling a little surprised, and even hurt, that he was still carrying it around. Then she reminded herself that she still had plenty of pictures of Seth kicking around. "I keep meaning to throw it away," Anders explained somewhat sheepishly.

Susanna studied the picture. Jennifer was definitely a knockout: long, dark, tangled curls; a body to die for; a big, self-confident smile. "She's pretty."

"Yes," agreed Anders. "She cared a lot about how she looked, about clothes and makeup and her exercise program. She kept track of her weight and measurements in a notebook."

Susanna laughed. "You're kidding!"

Anders smiled. "No."

"Doesn't sound like your type," Susanna observed.

"It is strange to think I ever was interested in Jennifer," Anders replied. He touched Susanna's cheek. "I know better now."

They kissed again. Then Anders looked earnestly into Susanna's eyes. "What about Seth? What was he like?"

Susanna flinched. It hadn't occurred to her that, naturally, Anders might be curious about her former love too. "Seth was . . ." Susanna stopped. Anders's question opened a door she preferred to keep shut. What had Carly said about living for today and not thinking about tomorrow? *I won't think about yesterday either,* Susanna determined. *I won't. I can't.*

With an effort of will, she blocked the images poised to pour forth from her memory. "Seth is dead," she said flatly. "I'd rather not talk about him."

"I'm sorry," Anders said.

"It's okay."

This time, the silence that fell over them felt

unnatural. Susanna reached out for Anders, obliterating the awkward moment with a hungry kiss. "I shouldn't have brought it up, asking about Jennifer," she whispered after a moment. "The past is the past. All I want to think about is right now."

But for the rest of the evening, they couldn't quite recapture the blissful mood they'd been in earlier. It was as if there were other ghostly presences with them in the car.

"It can't be a coincidence," Jin observed in the cafeteria a few days later, "that colleges mail out their acceptance and rejection letters on April Fools' Day."

"Tell me about it," Carly replied with feeling. "When I saw those three skinny envelopes in the mailbox yesterday, I almost croaked. I thought, 'Please, let this be somebody's idea of a joke.'"

The Altavista High senior class was in a collective state of high anxiety as they started hearing from the schools they'd applied to. A fat envelope meant you were in; a thin one wasn't such good news. Susanna and her friends had all received a few of each.

"You're accepted at your safety school," Kate reminded Carly, "so at least you won't be flipping burgers at the grill next year."

"And you're on the waiting list at Pomona. I'm sure you'll end up getting in," Susanna said encouragingly.

Carly sighed. "Easy for you to say, Suze. You know for a fact you'll be at Stanford in the fall. But I'll be in suspense for weeks and weeks." She held up her hands, forlornly inspecting her nails. "I've already chewed these down to stubs."

Susanna couldn't deny it had been an incredible relief to learn not only that she'd been accepted at Stanford, but that she'd won a Community Service Club scholarship too. Kate and her boyfriend, Doug Elliott, had both gotten into Berkeley, their first choice. Jin was still waiting to hear from Yale, but her hopes weren't high: She'd been turned down by a few other Ivies and would probably attend Wellesley College, an all-girls' school in Massachusetts.

"What about you, Anders?" Doug asked as he twisted the top off a bottle of iced tea. "How does the whole college thing work in Norway?"

Anders was sitting next to Susanna. They were holding hands under the table, and now he gave her fingers a squeeze. "I have known for a while that I am accepted to the university in Bergen," he told Doug. "I begin in September."

"Too bad you can't stay in the States," Doug commented.

"The *universitetet* provides a very good education," said Anders. "My friends from home will go there as well."

"But not Susanna," Carly interjected. "That's what Doug's getting at, right?"

Doug cocked one eyebrow sardonically. "Yes, Oh Tactful One."

Suddenly, Susanna had had enough of this particular topic of conversation. Releasing Anders's hand, she hopped to her feet. "Coffee, anyone?" she asked briskly.

Carly tagged along to the coffee bar. "It's not like it's news," she said, somewhat apologetically. "I mean, that Anders is going back to Norway."

"No, it's not," Susanna agreed, rummaging in her purse for some cash.

"It stinks, huh?"

"Yeah."

"You knew from the start, though."

"Right. We knew from the start."

As they waited for their café lattes, Carly leaned her elbows on the counter. "It's so totally weird, isn't it?" she mused in a melancholy tone. "After graduation, we'll all go our separate ways. You and Kate'll still be in the Bay Area, but with any luck, I'll be downstate at Pomona. And Jin's going to the East Coast!"

"We'll all come back to Altavista for vacations, though," Susanna pointed out.

"Right." Carly linked her arm through Susanna's. "The good-byes aren't forever. We'll always be friends."

Carly had cheered up, but all at once, Susanna lost her taste for café latte, or anything else. *I'll see my hometown friends again after graduation,* she thought, *but when I say good-bye to Anders, it* will *be forever. I'll never see him again.*

Walking back to the table, she kept her face carefully expressionless, hiding her distress. Because of Stanford, her friends assumed she was psyched about the future. She had so much to look forward to. But instead, she was filled with an all-too-familiar dread. *We knew better, Anders and I,* Susanna thought. It would have been safer to stay just friends. Then, when he left, the adjustment wouldn't have been so tough. She'd have been bummed for a few days, but the sadness would have passed, just a blip on the screen. It wouldn't change her life. Change it the way losing Seth had . . .

Anders had turned in his chair in order to watch her, his eyes full of love. Susanna smiled at him, her own heart swelling with emotion. *Don't think about tomorrow,* she counseled herself, repeating the advice like a mantra. *Don't think about tomorrow, don't think about tomorrow . . .*

Susanna sat down again. Instead of drinking her coffee, though, she held Anders's hand tightly, clingingly, as if she planned never to let go.

Anders stood next to the mailbox at the bottom of the Collinas' driveway, a stack of bills, magazines, and flyers in his hand. On top was an envelope addressed to him. The return address: Stanford University, Office of Admission.

Overhead, the April sky was clear and blue. A warm breeze rustled the leaves of the eucalyptus trees, wafting their spicy fragrance through the air. But for Anders, the afternoon seemed suddenly dark and cold. He could tell instantly that the envelope contained only a single sheet of paper, and it could only mean one thing.

Too bad, he thought morosely as he sauntered back to the house. He'd known it was a long shot, applying to such a prestigious American college; and until recently, he hadn't cared that much whether or not he got in. He missed Norway and couldn't wait to go back this summer. But since Susanna . . .

Anders started to crumple up the envelope from Stanford. Then, on second thought, he ripped it open and pulled out the letter. He expected to see the standard insincere opening sentence all the kids at school had joked about during lunch that day. "Thank you for applying to College X, but due to a record number of outstanding candidates, we regret to inform you that we are unable to offer you a place in next year's freshman class. . . ."

Anders stopped in his tracks. This letter was different. He skimmed it fast, then reread it more slowly to make sure he'd understood it properly. "'We have placed your name on the waiting list,'" Anders mumbled to himself, "'and will contact you as soon as possible if we are able to offer you a spot in the class of . . .'"

He dropped down on the porch steps, stunned. On the waiting list! Anders raked a hand through his hair, not at all certain what to think. Neither accepted nor rejected, but something in between.

He'd decided a while back not to mention to his American friends, not even Susanna, that he'd applied to Stanford. He figured that way, no one would need to know if he got turned down, but if he got in, he could surprise Susanna with the happy news. "What am I going to tell her now?" he wondered out loud.

He remembered how she'd reacted to the conversation at lunchtime when everyone was talking about college. She'd tried to appear upbeat, but Anders could tell she was upset inside. He too had been depressed thinking about returning to Bergen. But he'd harbored a secret hope: When he got home from school, he'd find a big, fat envelope from Stanford, an acceptance letter and everything that went with it. He'd announce to Susanna that instead of being separated by oceans and continents, for the next four years they'd be students together at Stanford.

The secret hope wasn't gone, but it was diminished. Anders folded the letter back up and lifted his eyes to the forested horizon, squinting in the bright afternoon sunshine. Should he tell Susanna, or was it just setting her—both of them—up for a heartbreaking fall? Was a small hope worse than none at all?

ELEVEN

A FEW AFTERNOONS later, Anders met Susanna at the A.H.S. playing fields after softball practice. Carly had wandered out from the locker room after swimming laps in the school pool. The three walked into town to share a pitcher of the Altavista Grill's famous homemade lemonade.

Scooting into the booth, Susanna eyed the plastic-covered menu standing between the salt-and-pepper shakers. After an intense workout, she was ravenous. "You know what would taste good with lemonade? A jumbo order of curly fries."

"No, onion rings," said Carly. "Or how about splitting a burger?"

Anders laughed. "This is the classic American approach to fitness. You exercise, which is good for you, and then you eat things that are not so good for you."

Susanna gave his leg a playful pinch. "Just because back in Norway you never eat anything but salmon and strawberries, Mr. Health Nut, doesn't mean you can't cheat a little while you're here."

"If they had salmon and strawberries on the menu, I'd order them in your honor," Carly told Anders. "But the grill only serves greasy fried stuff. So what'll it be?"

They decided on onion rings, which could qualify as a vegetable if need be, hold the burger. As the waitress headed off with their order, a tall, good-looking guy entered the restaurant. "Look, it's Brad!" Susanna hissed to Carly.

Carly swiveled in her seat. Brad spotted her just as she spotted him. They exchanged shy waves. When Carly didn't say anything, Susanna took it upon herself to call out, "Hi, Brad. Want to join us?"

Carly kicked her under the table. "Too late," Susanna whispered. Brad was already on his way over.

He slid into the booth next to Carly. Carly was blushing profusely. "What's up?" Brad said to no one in particular.

Susanna got busy drinking her lemonade so that Carly would have to answer. "Oh," said Carly, pushing a wavy strand of blond hair back from her face. "Uh, not much. You know. Same old, same old."

Brad nodded solemnly as if she'd imparted some actual information. "Yeah. Sure. Right."

Susanna decided they needed some help getting the conversational ball rolling. "So, Brad. The baseball team's having a great season."

As well as being an up-and-coming star on the A.H.S. football team, Brad was a varsity first baseman.

"Yep," he conceded. "There are some terrific players this year. We had a squeaker the other day, though, that game against San Stefano."

"That game was incredible," Carly burst out. "That double play you and Michael made in the tenth inning—"

She stopped short, turning pink again. Susanna knew Carly hadn't meant to let slip that she'd happened to be in the bleachers at every single one of Brad's home games.

"You saw that?" Brad said, clearly pleased. "Yeah, well . . ." He shrugged modestly. "It came at a good time. I was glad to help the team."

"You did more than help," Carly told him. "You also batted in the winning run!"

"That was just making up for the previous game in Pacific Point when I went zero-for-three," Brad said.

While Susanna and Anders polished off the onion rings and lemonade, Carly and Brad chattered, bouncing energetically from one topic to another. They hardly noticed when Susanna and Anders exchanged an expressive glance, then stood up abruptly. "Gotta run," Susanna announced. "See you!"

Outside on the sidewalk, she and Anders strolled hand in hand, laughing about Carly and Brad. "I've never seen two people more infatuated with each other," Susanna remarked. "Except for you and me, of course."

Anders squeezed her hand. "They could be the second-best couple at Altavista High."

"If Carly would just get over her hang-up about their age difference," Susanna agreed. "If she has any sense, she's asking him to the senior prom right this minute."

"That reminds me," said Anders. "Will you . . ." He cleared his throat. "Ahem. Would you do me the honor . . . what I'm trying to say is, *kommer du med meg på dansen?*"

Susanna blinked up at him. "What?"

Anders tried again. "The prom. We talked about it a long time ago, remember? When it was just going to be for show. That we should go together. But now . . . I know it is the most important night of the year for seniors at A.H.S., and I would like to spend it with you."

"Oh, Anders." Right there on Main Street, Susanna flung her arms around his neck. "Of course I'll go to the prom with you! I was already assuming we would."

They resumed walking, this time with their arms around each other's waists. "You need to rent a tuxedo, you know," Susanna informed him.

"Really?" he teased. "In Norway, we wear blue jeans to formal occasions."

She hip checked him. "*And* you have to reserve a limousine. *And* order a corsage from the florist. It should match my dress."

"The corsage or the limousine?"

"Which I haven't bought yet," Susanna continued, "but when I do, I'll tell you the color. And dinner reservations! That's your job too."

Anders slapped his palm against his forehead. "I do not know if I can remember so many responsibilities. Maybe you should write a list for me."

As they walked along joking about the prom, Susanna couldn't remember when she'd been in such a lighthearted mood. Living for today definitely made things easier, changing her whole outlook. *I'll look ahead as far as the prom, but I won't think about what comes after,* Susanna decided. It was the only way.

"You asked *who* to the prom?" exclaimed Susanna the next afternoon, gaping at Carly.

Susanna, Carly, Jin, and Kate were driving into San Francisco to shop for prom dresses. As Jin's Mazda zipped over the Golden Gate Bridge, Carly answered nonchalantly, "Colin Van Etten. Why are you so shocked?"

"Because just yesterday—at the grill—you and Brad," Susanna spluttered.

Carly finished polishing her sunglasses on her T-shirt and stuck them back on her nose. "Oh, right. It was fun running into him. He's a real sweetheart. But then last night Colin called, and, you know, like, I couldn't believe that he'd really want to go with me to a silly old prom now that he's in college, but he said he'd be psyched for it."

Kate twisted in the front passenger seat so she could give Carly the eye. "I thought you said, now that you've gone out with him a couple of times, that he's kind of on the boring side? Like majorly self-involved?"

"Yeah, a male version of Alicia," Jin tossed out.

Carly shrugged. "He's a little on the superficial side, yeah, sure," she conceded. "But he's also cool and outrageously good-looking."

"And that matters more than being nice and fun to be with?" wondered Susanna.

"I wish you wouldn't keep harping on the Brad thing," Carly lectured Susanna. "I've told you a zillion times, he's too young for me. Maybe I'll reconsider the situation ten years from now when I'm twenty-eight and he's twenty-six."

"But it's just logistics," Susanna argued.

Carly blinked. "What?"

"You and Brad. When I was worried about getting involved with Anders, since he's from another country, you said to follow my heart and forget about the logistics."

"Did I say that?"

"You sure did."

"Well." Carly considered this. "I don't think it's true; I must have said it just to make you feel better."

"Gee, thanks," said Susanna dryly.

"You'll be sorry, Carly," Kate predicted. "There's only one senior prom, and when you're yawning your way through a slow dance with Colin Van Etten, you'll wish you were with someone you really cared about."

Susanna thought about Kate's remark as the girls disappeared into dressing rooms at Nuevo Mundo, a trendy boutique near Union Square in San Francisco. *"You'll wish you were with someone you really cared about. . . ."*

She wiggled into a sleeveless coral pink dress that fit snugly over her hips and then flared out into a flouncy short skirt. She could hear Carly and Jin buzzing down the hall. "If you pile your hair on top of your head like this," Carly was saying, "and then add a sprig of baby's breath . . ."

The coral dress fit perfectly and really brought out her suntan and the depths of her eyes, but suddenly, for some reason, Susanna couldn't get fired up about it. Trying on dresses made the prom seem too real, too close. And the closer the prom got, the closer she and Anders got to good-bye.

Tears stung Susanna's eyes. Kate was extremely smart and full of common sense and was nearly always right about things, but on this particular subject . . . *It would almost be better to go to the dance with someone I don't care about,* Susanna thought glumly as she unzipped the dress and slipped it back on its hanger. Or maybe even not go at all.

"Hey, Susanna!"

Susanna and Anders were walking to the student parking lot after school when someone called out behind them. Susanna turned. Leslie Fisher, the school yearbook editor, waved at them frantically. "Glad I caught you," she panted, hurrying up. "Boy, am I disorganized. And we still have so much work to do on the yearbook! I don't know how we'll ever get it finished."

"Is there something I can do to help?" Susanna asked.

"It's just Seth's page," Leslie said. "We thought we'd put it at the beginning of the senior-class section. Photographs and people's memories of him. You and I talked about it a long time ago, remember?"

Seth's page. Susanna felt as if she'd been punched in the stomach. "I remember," she said slowly.

"You must have a lot of pictures," Leslie went on. "Would you pick out a special one? I'm telling his other friends to stick something in the yearbook office mail slot by Friday."

Susanna bit her lip, then nodded. "I can do that."

"You could help lay out the page too, if you want. We'd appreciate your input."

Susanna shook her head. "No," she said, her voice growing even more strained. "No, you go ahead and do it. I'm sure you'll do a great job."

"Thanks, Susanna." Leslie gave her a warm smile. "Well, see you. See you, Anders."

Leslie bustled off. Susanna stared after her, still feeling stunned and a little bit sick. Anders touched her arm. "Are you all right?" he asked quietly.

Susanna turned back to him, pasting a false smile on her face. "Of course," she chirped. "Why wouldn't I be?"

"You just looked . . . upset," he ventured. "By this yearbook thing."

"Not at all."

"Are you sure you don't want to talk?"

"I'm fine," Susanna insisted. She jingled her car keys. "So, where do you want to go? Beach or mountains?"

As they drove away from the high school, Susanna cranked the volume on the radio so that further conversation was impossible. She knew Anders wanted to understand how she felt about something like Seth's memorial page, but she refused to enter that territory. *Leslie caught me off guard,* Susanna thought, *but it won't happen again.* She simply would not let herself be ambushed by old memories.

"Are you sure you want to come in with me?" Susanna asked Anders as she parked her car at the hospital the following afternoon. "It's a beautiful day. You could be hiking or something."

"I want to meet these kids you always talk about." He grinned. "And also, I am *very* artistic."

She smiled. "I didn't know that."

"It is true—you will see. I brought some photos of home for showing the kids how to paint scenes of Norway."

Susanna shifted her art portfolio to her other hand so she could hug him around the waist as they walked along. "I'm sure they'll really like that."

As usual, Susanna paused to greet the nurses and residents, introducing everyone to Anders. Bob the intern wriggled his sandy eyebrows at her. "So this is why we don't see you around so much anymore, eh?" he kidded.

"I haven't missed a single art therapy session," Susanna protested.

"Just teasing you." Bob put a playful headlock

on Susanna, rumpling her hair. "Take good care of her, fella," he advised Anders.

The Ward F patients' lounge was crowded with expectant children, as usual. Susanna had figured the kids would take to Anders after some initial shyness, but she was amazed at how quickly he won them over. Within minutes, he was the center of a lively group jockeying to get close to watch him reproduce a dramatic scene of a Norwegian fjord using neon Crayola markers.

Susanna stayed off to the side, perched on the arm of an easy chair. Watching from a distance gave her a perspective on the scene that she didn't usually have. *Becky's lost more weight,* she observed, an anxious feeling in her gut. But little Danny! He looked healthier than she'd ever seen him. The bone marrow transplant had been a success.

Yes, it looked like Danny was going to make it. But what about Becky? And Marcus? On the way in, Karen had told Susanna that he'd been transferred to the pediatric intensive care unit. His prognosis wasn't good. *There's no guarantee,* Susanna thought. Even with the best-trained doctors, the most dedicated nursing, and the most modern medical techniques. Even on art therapy day, it was impossible to forget that Ward F was a battlefield, and sometimes cancer won.

Suddenly, a tidal wave of anger and sorrow surged up and rolled over her, tumbling her in its treacherous surf. The wave had started to build the day before, when Leslie approached Susanna about the yearbook memorial page. Now the familiar smell of the hospital, the color of the paint on the walls, a nurse's voice over the intercom all combined into a potent, evocative force. The locked door to Susanna's memories of Seth's illness and death swung wide open.

The unfairness, the randomness! Of all the people in the world, why did Seth have to get sick? And why did he have to die when other people were cured? Susanna dug her fingernails into the chair's upholstery, remembering. At first he'd responded so well to the chemotherapy. Everyone's hopes had risen like helium balloons at a birthday party. She and Seth started making plans for the summer. They'd backpack and camp and maybe go on a white-water rafting trip. . . .

Then, abruptly, his condition worsened. Despite chemo, the tumor kept growing. Susanna recalled how she'd sat through classes at A.H.S. at the beginning of the school year, unable to focus on her teachers' words, the scribbles on the blackboard. She'd handed in homework and taken tests and written papers without even realizing what she was doing, just going through the motions like a robot. Every single day after school, and all day on weekends, she went to the hospital where Seth was fighting off one infection after another, growing weaker and weaker. Strong, wiry Seth who could carry a sixty-pound backpack with ease, who could jog ten miles and hardly break a sweat.

Susanna had turned her face away so the

children wouldn't see her blot her tears on the sleeve of her shirt. The onslaught of emotions had left her feeling helpless and drained. As she turned blurry eyes back to Anders, he glanced over and flashed her a smile. She forced herself to smile back, trying to push her feelings of grief back under the surface. She'd been able to keep them there the night before, when she'd picked out a picture of Seth for the yearbook page. But this time, they wouldn't go. She couldn't stop thinking about Seth, remembering every moment of the long, indescribably painful process of losing him.

Susanna had thought her heart was healed, but the wound was still red and raw. *How could I have been so stupid?* she wondered dully. How could she have fallen for someone else who was going to leave her?

She finished out the art therapy session, just barely managing to hold herself together until she pulled her Civic into the Collinas' driveway to drop off Anders. Then, her hands still gripping the steering wheel, she started to cry, and once she started, she couldn't stop.

"Susanna," Anders said, his eyes filled with concern. "What is the matter?"

Hot tears streamed down Susanna's cheeks. She shook her head, unable to speak.

"Susanna," he repeated. He placed a firm, gentle hand on her arm. "Tell me why you are sad."

"I can't . . . I can't . . ." she stammered. Shaking off his hand, she flung open the door and stumbled out of the car.

There was no place to go, so she just stood in the driveway, her hands pressed against her face, sobbing. Anders hurried over to her and folded her in his arms. "It is okay," he said soothingly.

Susanna pushed him away again. "It's *not* okay," she cried out. "Don't you see, Anders? It's not going to work."

He frowned. "What do you mean?"

"I mean, it's not going to work," Susanna repeated, her voice cracking. "Us. You and me."

"I do not understand," he said hoarsely.

They were the hardest words she'd ever uttered in her life. "I'm—I'm breaking up with you."

"Breaking up?"

"We have to stop seeing each other."

Anders turned pale. "But why?"

"Because I can't handle it," Susanna choked out. "At the hospital just now, it all came back to me. How it felt. It's terrible to be left behind. Remember when Jennifer left you?"

"Yes, but—"

"I can't just wait around for you to go. So I'm leaving now before . . ." Her voice dropped to a ragged whisper. "Before I end up caring for you too much."

"Please, Susanna." Anders reached toward her. "You—I—I don't want to . . . *Jeg orker ikke tanken på å miste deg.*"

She couldn't bear to watch him struggling to find the words in English; it was better to not know what he was really trying to say. Racing back to the car, she jumped into the driver's seat and slammed the door.

"Susanna, wait!" Anders shouted.

Susanna revved the engine, drowning him out. Shifting into reverse, she stepped on the gas. Dust billowed as she backed up the car.

On the road, she shifted into first. As she sped away, she glimpsed Anders through the side window. He stood alone in the driveway, his shoulders slumped and his arms hanging limp at his sides. In the dappled sun and shadows, it was hard to tell, but she was pretty sure his face was wet with tears.

Her own tears continued to flow. She couldn't believe what she'd just done. She was crazy about Anders, and she'd broken up with him!

But what was the alternative? To let herself fall wholeheartedly in love with a boy who'd move back to Norway in just a month? "It's better this way," Susanna tried tearfully to convince herself, even though the ache in her heart contradicted her reasoning. "It's better this way."

TWELVE

"I HATE THE feeling that everyone's looking at me," Susanna said to Carly a few days later. She clutched her books a little closer to her chest as she plowed her way down the crowded hallway toward the cafeteria.

"That's the way it goes," Carly responded pragmatically. "You and Anders are this week's big breakup. Front-page news."

"Don't people have anything better to talk about?" Susanna complained.

"Nope."

It was a beautiful day, so the two girls opted to spend lunch period outdoors. Susanna knew there was less chance of running into Anders that way, and she was doing her best to avoid him. Choosing a sunny corner of the courtyard, she dropped her books with a thud, then flung herself down on the grass beside them.

"Aren't you going to eat anything?" Carly asked before biting into her chicken salad sandwich.

Susanna stretched out on her back, her head pillowed on her books, and closed her eyes. "I'm not hungry."

"You're the one who broke up with him. You're not supposed to be moping."

Susanna didn't comment.

"He's moping too, you know," Carly volunteered after a moment.

"He is?" Susanna said, hoping she didn't sound too interested.

"Majorly. Poor guy."

Susanna swallowed. She was so caught up in her own pain, she'd practically forgotten that Anders would be suffering too.

"It's really a shame," Carly went on. "You bought that totally hot dress, and now you won't get a chance to wear it."

Susanna didn't point out that the dress was the least of it. "I'll return it."

"Guess I'll return mine too, then," Carly said with a sigh.

Susanna sat up. "How come?"

"Didn't I tell you?" Carly wrinkled her nose ruefully. "I blew off Colin this past weekend."

"No way!"

"Yes way."

"What happened?"

Carly wrapped up the remaining half of her sandwich. "Nothing hugely dramatic. He invited me into the city for this party on campus. The night had all the right ingredients, you know? Cool college party with an excellent live band, great-looking date . . ." Carly heaved another sigh. "I was bored to tears. When Colin tried to kiss me, I actually yawned!"

Susanna laughed. "That bad?"

"I started picturing myself going into a coma at the prom, so right then and there, I told him I'd changed my mind about it. He wasn't exactly upset. I must bore him a little too."

"So now we're both dateless," Susanna observed. She held out a hand, and Carly passed her the second half of the chicken salad sandwich. "Pathetic, eh?"

"I suppose we should cancel our hair and manicure appointments."

"No way," Carly declared. "We still deserve to treat ourselves."

"And get all beautiful just for each other?"

"Why not?"

Susanna wasn't sure whether the prospect made her feel more like laughing or crying. "Oh, Carly," she said. "How did we get ourselves into this one?"

"Talent, I guess."

Carly pulled a notebook out of her book bag and started doing the French homework that was due next period. Susanna munched the sandwich, her face pensive. *Senior year,* she mused. It was supposed to be unforgettable, and it certainly had been for her, but in the wrong way. For a while, with Anders, she'd been happy—incredibly so—

but now as she looked back on the past year, it seemed in general to have gone from bad to worse. *I'll be sitting home on prom night thinking about two boys who've gone out of my life. I can't wait for this horrible year to end.*

After dinner, Anders excused himself from the table and went outside. He had a lot of home-work—final exams were coming up—but he wasn't in the mood to study. He was only in the mood to rock in the Collinas' backyard hammock and think about how much he missed Susanna.

To top it all off, he'd phoned the Stanford admission office that afternoon. The woman who took the call said she couldn't tell him anything about the status of his application. Stanford still hadn't made a decision about him, and in Anders's opinion, that meant it was safe to assume the worst.

He'd been in the hammock for an hour, looking up at the treetops and watching the sky change from robin's egg blue to purple, when Mrs. Collina appeared in the twilight. "Nice night," she said, pulling up a lawn chair. "Mind if I join you?"

"Please do," Anders said politely.

She sat for a minute admiring the sunset, then said gently, "Anders, I hope you won't think I'm being nosy, but lately you seem . . . distracted. Is something bothering you?"

Anders shrugged, embarrassed. "It is nothing," he assured Mrs. Collina. "I think I am just . . ." He remembered the term Susanna had taught him the day they met in the state park. "Homesick."

"You know that if you ever need to talk . . . I think of you as one of my own boys now."

Anders gave her a grateful smile. "Thank you. I am okay."

Mrs. Collina patted his knee, then stood up. Before turning to go, she handed him an envelope. "Here. This came for you in today's mail."

Taking the letter, Anders sat up in the hammock. As Mrs. Collina walked away, he read the return address. The letter was from Beverly Hills.

It was from Jennifer.

As his eyes trailed Mrs. Collina back to the house, Anders smiled grimly at the irony. After all this time, he'd finally heard from Jennifer! He would have loved getting a letter from her a few months ago, but now she was the last thing on his mind.

Inside, Anders tore the letter in half without even opening it and tossed it into the trash. He wasn't in the least bit curious about what it might contain. He didn't want to read about Jennifer's life. Susanna was the only one he cared about.

Susanna pulled her desk chair up to her bedroom window and sat with her elbows propped on the sill, staring glumly outward. As usual, the weather was gorgeous. May was one of the nicest months in Marin County—long, clear days with no fog. Softball practice had been short and light because they had a game the next day, and it was a perfect afternoon for mountain biking or walking

140

on the beach. But Susanna didn't have the heart for any of the activities she used to do with Anders. It was far more satisfying to sit inside and sulk.

Not that she'd admit to herself that she was sulking. *I don't miss him,* she thought as she opened the Flaubert novel she was reading for French class. *I did the right thing, breaking up with him. My life is a lot less complicated now.* She ignored the other voice in her head, the one that said, *A lot less complicated, perhaps, but a lot more lonely.*

After reading three pages without absorbing a single word, Susanna slammed her book shut. Taking a hint from her grumbling stomach, she shuffled to the kitchen to scrounge up a snack. Then, bagel and cream cheese in hand, she headed out the back door.

It was Dr. Reyes's day off from the clinic, and she was working in her vegetable garden. Without looking up, she beckoned to Susanna. "Help me transplant these seedlings," she invited.

Susanna kicked off her clogs and padded barefoot down the garden path, enjoying the warmth of the soil between her toes. Kneeling next to her mother in the dirt, she got busy digging little holes for the baby lettuce, tomato, squash, and bean plants.

"I'm surprised to find you home on a day like this," Dr. Reyes remarked, tamping the earth around a head of leafy green lettuce.

"I have a ton of homework," Susanna said.

"Did you and Anders have a fight? I haven't seen him in a while."

"We didn't have a fight . . . exactly." Susanna plucked a weed from the dirt, then lobbed it into the nearby wheelbarrow. "We just kind of . . . broke up."

Dr. Reyes sat back on her heels, brushing a strand of fair hair off her forehead with the back of her wrist. "Oh, honey. Why didn't you say something?"

"It's not that big a deal," Susanna mumbled. "I mean, we only went on a couple of dates, really."

"But you were such good friends."

Susanna shrugged. "It wasn't meant to be."

Dr. Reyes turned back to the garden. Taking another tiny lettuce from its pot, she placed it in the ground. "Well, I'm sorry. He was a nice boy."

Susanna's throat constricted. The note of regret in her mother's voice made her want to bawl like a baby. Instead, she snapped crabbily, "Being nice isn't the only thing that matters. As a boyfriend, Anders had some major shortcomings."

"Like what?"

"Like being Norwegian."

"I thought that made him interesting," said Dr. Reyes.

"Have you looked at a world atlas lately, Mom?"

Dr. Reyes nodded thoughtfully. "I see your point."

For a few minutes, they worked side by side in silence. Susanna was relieved that they'd gotten the Anders discussion over with. Talking about him made the pain in her heart throb anew.

When all the heads of lettuce were transplanted in a neat row, Dr. Reyes started in on the tomatoes.

"I had a tough day at the migrant workers' clinic yesterday," she said.

"Yeah?"

"Sent a woman to the cancer ward. Malignant melanoma—the worst kind of skin cancer. She's young, married, two little kids."

"Will she die?"

"Almost certainly."

Susanna couldn't imagine anything more depressing. She stared at her mother, for an instant forgetting her own problems. "How do you stand it, Mom?"

"Sometimes it's really hard." Dr. Reyes sighed heavily. "Usually, I have the satisfaction of seeing people get better, but in cases like this . . . I try to detach myself somewhat. I couldn't do my job otherwise. But I still get emotionally involved. Some of my patients become friends. I mourn the ones I can't save."

Susanna hadn't thought much lately about the dream she used to have about becoming a doctor and doing medical research. She wasn't sure anymore that she was cut out for the profession. "It would be better if you could just turn off your feelings, become a robot," she commented.

Dr. Reyes didn't answer for a long moment. Then she said quietly, "I wouldn't want to be numb to human feeling, even if it made my job easier. I love people. That's why I became a physician in the first place."

All at once, Susanna realized they weren't just talking about her mother's work. Under the surface,

Susanna's breakup with Anders was still on both their minds. And so was something—someone—else. Seth.

"I know what you're thinking, Mom," Susanna said, her voice catching on a sob. "But saying good-bye to Anders on top of everything else—graduation, all the changes that are coming up . . . I can't go through that a second time."

"You have to do what feels right," Dr. Reyes agreed. She looked deep into her daughter's eyes, her own eyes warm with compassion. "You have to take care of yourself. There's another way to think about it, though. It was awful to lose Seth. But if you could choose, would you rather never have known and loved him?"

Susanna stared back at her mother. Dr. Reyes didn't seem to expect an answer, which was just as well because Susanna couldn't have given her one. Turning away blindly, she dug the trowel into the soft earth. Then she just knelt on the dirt with the tender seedling cupped in her hands.

After stopping her bike outside the gate, Susanna hesitated, the somewhat wilted bouquet of wildflowers dangling from her hand. She hadn't been to the cemetery in months—not since the day she'd stopped there with Anders. *Why am I here?* she wondered. *What's the point? Seth's gone; he can't help me. He can't give me the answers.*

She turned away, fiddling with the kickstand on her bike, then looked back at the graveyard. The caretaker had just mown the lawn, and the air was perfumed with the sweetness of fresh-cut grass. A light breeze made the flowers planted by the head-stones bob and sway. It was a quiet, peaceful place—as good a spot as any to sit and think, Susanna decided. She pushed open the gate.

There was a new pot of geraniums on Seth's grave; his parents had been there recently, Susanna guessed. She dropped her own offering next to the flowerpot, then sat down cross-legged a few feet away.

"Hi, Seth," she said awkwardly after a minute. She glanced over her shoulder to make sure she was alone in the cemetery. "How's it going?"

She listened to the breeze, the birds singing, try-ing hard to remember what Seth's voice had sounded like. Suddenly, she felt as if she could hear it, hear his laughter.

"I don't know what to do, Seth," she whispered. "I'm so unhappy. And it's all your fault!"

Susanna was surprised by the anger that surged up inside her. As quickly as it came, though, it melted away, leaving her once again empty and sad. She buried her face in her hands. "No, it's not," she said, sniffling. "You didn't want to leave me. You didn't want to die. Oh, Seth. If you were still here, and I was gone, how would *you* feel?"

He couldn't tell her, of course. But Susanna re-alized she knew the answer anyway. She knew it because she'd known Seth.

We had so much fun because he was never in a bad mood, Susanna remembered. *He was so optimistic; he never let himself get frustrated and disappointed when things didn't go the way he wanted them to.* That was probably what she remembered most clearly about him. Up until the very end, he kept on searching for the silver lining in the clouds. He'd looked ahead to the future even when it grew apparent that he didn't *have* a future. As he lay in that hospital bed, so weak he could barely hold Susanna's hand, he was still talking about the things they'd do together, the places they'd go.

Susanna had been weeping quietly. Now she dried her eyes. In the past ten minutes, nothing about the world had changed. The sun was still shining; birds continued to chirp and squabble; the geraniums remained the warm pink color of salmon; there was still an old bleach stain shaped like a whale on the leg of her denim shorts. But inside, Susanna felt like a different person.

Seth, who'd loved life so much, who'd loved *her* so much, wouldn't have wanted her to be afraid of the future. She recalled his encouragement as she'd scaled the cables at Half Dome. *"Go for it, Suze! You can do it. Straight to the top!"*

Susanna stretched out a hand. For a brief moment, her fingertips brushed the warm stone where his name was carved. "Thanks, Seth," she whispered.

THIRTEEN

Back home, Susanna went straight to her bedroom. Taking the quilt-covered photo album from her nightstand drawer, she held it for a moment without opening it. She didn't need to look at the pictures in order to recollect each one in perfect detail. She would never forget Seth's face and all the good times they'd shared.

But it was time, she decided, to put the memories away. Going to her closet, she removed a cardboard box. Inside were other keepsakes from her relationship with Seth: more snapshots, a handful of postcards, a baseball cap, concert ticket stubs, a dried corsage, the necklace he'd given her for her birthday. After adding the photo album to the collection, Susanna taped the box shut and returned it to the back of the closet.

If she'd done this even just a month ago, she knew she would have felt guilty and disloyal, as if she were being unfaithful to Seth's memory. But now the gesture made her feel free. Getting over Seth's death had been like climbing an incredibly steep mountain. At last, she'd reached the top. After long miles of staring down at the rocky path under her feet, she could see blue sky and open space. She could see the future.

And I want my future to include Anders, Susanna realized.

There was a guide on national parks on Susanna's desk. When she opened it, a photograph slipped from between the pages—a snapshot she'd taken of Anders one day at the beach. Susanna propped the picture against the lamp on her night table. She didn't have a frame for it yet, but she'd get around to that. One step at a time.

All of a sudden, Susanna couldn't wait another minute to talk things over with Anders. Grabbing the telephone on her desk, she started to punch in the Collinas' number. She hung up before she'd finished dialing. She couldn't say what she needed to say over the phone—she had to see him in person.

I'll drive over there right now, Susanna decided. *I'll apologize for hurting his feelings and for wasting time when every single day we have left before he goes back to Bergen is so precious.*

Then Susanna smiled to herself. She could rehearse a long, flowery, passionate "I'm sorry" speech if she wanted, but three simple words would do the trick just as well or better. "I love you"— that said it all.

*　　*　　*

"'Dear Susanna,'" Anders murmured out loud, writing the words on a clean sheet of notebook paper. "'I know you do not want to see me anymore, but I very much believe that—'"

"No," he muttered. "That is not right." He scratched out the last few words, then crumpled the whole sheet up into a ball and tossed it into the wastebasket.

Smoothing a blank page, he tried again. "'Dear Susanna, We have been very good friends, and therefore it is not right that we should now end up to be not very good friends.'" Anders frowned at the clumsy sentence. "It is awful," he declared, crumpling up this page too.

Propping his elbows on the desk, he planted his chin in his hands with a discontented sigh. If he hoped to change Susanna's mind about going out with him, it was very important that he express himself correctly, but all of a sudden, he felt as if he'd completely lost his command of the English language. *If only I could write to her in Norwegian!* he thought.

In the distance, he heard the sound of the doorbell. Ignoring it, he began yet another letter to Susanna. This time, he wrote three whole sentences before tearing it to shreds.

The doorbell jingled again. Anders pushed his chair back, irritated. Mark was home too, but apparently his stereo was cranked so loud that he couldn't hear the bell.

Then a possibility occurred to Anders, making

his heart leap. Maybe it was Susanna! Maybe, like him, she'd been miserable since their breakup. The thought propelled Anders forward; he bounded down the stairs three at a time.

In the front hall, he slowed down, suddenly dry-mouthed with nervousness. What if it *was* Susanna? What would he say? Every single English word and rule of grammar he'd ever learned was scrambled in his brain like an omelette. Then Anders relaxed. He didn't need to remember much, just the three most important words in English or any other language: I love you.

He pulled the door open, his eyes bright with hope. Sure enough, there was a girl standing on the front step. She'd started to turn away, as if concluding that no one was home. Now she faced forward again and, when she saw Anders, flashed a brilliant smile.

He expected to see a beautiful girl. This girl was undeniably beautiful, but she was also dark-haired, petite, and curvy, whereas Susanna was tall, blond, and athletic.

Anders's jaw dropped.

"Surprise!" said Jennifer Nelson.

Her heart singing, Susanna drove along the winding country road that led to the Collinas' house, resisting the urge to speed around the sharp curves. *Wait till I tell Carly, Jin, and Kate,* she thought, coasting down a hill. *I'll be going to the senior prom after all!*

And then there was graduation to get ready for. Jin's parents were planning a celebration brunch before the ceremony at the high school. *Maybe I'll throw a party that night,* Susanna considered. The thought of graduating didn't depress her anymore. It really was all in how you looked at things, and graduation was a beginning as well as an end.

Half a mile later, she tapped the brakes. Anders's host family lived just around this bend. Three more mailboxes . . .

Susanna slowed down a little more. At the bottom of the Collinas' driveway, she stopped.

As she was about to pull into the driveway, her heart gave a bound. Anders was standing on the walk in front of the house, almost as if he'd been expecting her. A millisecond later, though, Susanna noticed something else that sent her heart tumbling down into her sneakers.

Anders wasn't alone. An attractive, dark-haired girl stood next to him, and the pair was deep in conversation. *Jennifer!* Susanna guessed with a sickening jolt of recognition.

At first, Susanna wasn't going to assume the worst. Jennifer was an old girlfriend, but that didn't necessarily mean anything. But then, as Susanna watched in dismay, Jennifer flung her arms around Anders, and he returned the embrace unhesitatingly.

For an endless, agonizing moment, Susanna was frozen with shock, unable to move. Then she recovered herself. *I can't let them see me,* she thought, stepping hard on the clutch and shifting into first gear. She accelerated fast, praying that Anders and Jennifer hadn't noticed the car. She needn't have

151

worried. As she cast one last glance in the rearview mirror, she could see that the couple was still in what appeared to be a totally passionate clinch.

Susanna retraced her route back home. Luckily, she knew the way well, because she could hardly see where she was going. Tears fogged her eyes, and her breath came in ragged, sobbing gasps.

The whole time she'd been confronting her emotions about loss, life, and love, Anders had been pursuing another agenda. Not that long ago, he'd told her that he loved her more than he'd loved Jennifer, but obviously he'd changed his mind. For all she knew, he'd never even taken that picture of Jennifer out of his wallet.

It didn't take him long to get over me, Susanna thought, a knifelike pain piercing her heart.

She was alone again.

FOURTEEN

"H E SURE DIDN'T waste any time," Kate declared with a snort of disgust.

"He must have phoned her like the *minute* you two broke up," Carly deduced.

"You're way better off without him," Jin agreed, patting Susanna's hand.

The four girls had gathered around the kitchen table at Carly's house for an emergency support session. Susanna smiled at her friends through her tears. "Thanks, guys. It really helps to vent, you know?"

"This will help too," Carly predicted, taking a plastic grocery bag from the freezer and dumping it on the table. Four cartons of ice cream tumbled out.

"Four?" observed Jin in disbelief.

"One pint for each of us," Carly explained. Jin continued to shake her head. "Well, I had to buy everybody's favorite flavor!"

Carly passed out spoons. They commenced

eating ice cream straight from the cartons. "Men," Kate pronounced after a minute.

"Can't live with 'em," Jin said.

"Can't live without 'em," Carly concluded.

Susanna sniffled. "I just feel so *stupid*. I really thought I knew him. I thought he was a different kind of person. I believed him when he told me that he—he . . ." Her eyes brimmed.

"I guess he turned out to be as fickle as what's-her-name," Kate said.

Jin licked some ice cream from her spoon. "Those two deserve each other."

"He was always a major flirt," Carly remarked.

Susanna didn't completely agree, but she let it pass. Her friends were just trying to make her feel better, and it was working, a little.

"Ugh. If I finish this whole carton, I'll shoot myself," Kate said. Sticking the top back on, she pushed the ice cream toward the center of the table. "So, here's my idea, Suze. Doug has this terrific friend from marching band, Jonathan Pratt. You know Jonathan—plays the trumpet? Well, he doesn't have a date for the prom yet, but I happen to know he'd love to take you if you're interested. We could double!"

"Jonathan's cute," Carly contributed.

"Actually," Jin interjected, "I was thinking about fixing Susanna up with Kenny's friend Malcolm. Mal's always had a crush on you, Suze. He'd be delirious if you went to the prom with him. And then *we* could double!"

154

"Hey," said Carly, sticking out her lower lip in a pout. "How come no one wants to double with *me*?"

Susanna spoke up. "You guys are really sweet to think of me. I appreciate it, but . . ." She stared down at the carton of ice cream she hadn't touched. "I can't go to the dance with Jonathan *or* Malcolm. I just can't."

"Are you sure?" Kate asked.

Susanna nodded.

Kate didn't press her, and neither did the others. When they were done eating ice cream, they adjourned to the family room, where Carly popped a movie into the VCR—a silly comedy. Susanna sat on the sofa, clutching a throw pillow to her stomach, and made a point of laughing when everyone else did; but inside, she still felt like crying. She was surrounded by her very best friends in the whole world, but she'd never felt more lonely.

Anders was still in a daze. He'd borrowed Mrs. Collina's car and taken Jennifer out to dinner at a restaurant in Sonoma where he was fairly sure he wouldn't run into anyone from Altavista High School. Now, sitting across the table from Jennifer, he tried to get a grip on himself and untangle his tongue. Luckily, she didn't seem to mind doing most of the talking.

"I can't believe you were so surprised to see me," Jennifer exclaimed, tossing her glossy black hair over one shoulder. "Didn't you get my letter?"

155

Anders remembered the letter he'd torn up and thrown away without reading. "Uh . . ."

"It must have gotten lost in the mail. So you don't even know about what happened with Bill! *Well.*" She laughed. "I'll have to tell you the whole story, huh?"

"Er . . ."

"It was pretty devastating, actually." Jennifer grew somber. "I mean, breaking up the night of our senior prom. You can *imagine.*"

"Yes," Anders managed.

"It was supposed to be such a wonderful night." Jennifer sighed sadly. "Now my prom memories will always be totally depressing."

"I'm sorry," Anders said, opening and then closing his menu.

"Don't be." Jennifer was smiling again. "You know what? Bill had been acting like a real jerk. He totally took me for granted. I don't need that, you know? I deserve someone who appreciates me." She reached across the table and squeezed his hand. "Someone like you," she added softly. "You even wrote to me after I treated you so badly."

Anders stiffened. "Jennifer, there's something I should tell—"

"*Don't* say you have another girlfriend!" Jennifer exclaimed.

"Well, not at the moment, but—"

"Good. Then we can pick up right where we left off. Oh, sure," she continued at a pace that left Anders breathless, "I know you're going back to

Norway, and I'll only be staying with my cousins in San Francisco for a week." She gave him a flirtatious smile. "But we can have a lot of fun in a week, don't you think?"

Anders turned red. "Jennifer, you're getting the wrong idea."

"About what?"

"About me. About . . . us."

She pursed her full, red lips in a tiny frown. "What do you mean?"

"I mean . . ." Anders stared at Jennifer, trying to remember what it had been like to be in love with her. He felt as if that had happened to another Anders, in another lifetime. Jennifer was just as she'd always been: vivacious, magnetic, beautiful. All qualities that had charmed him then, but now they weren't enough.

"Jennifer, I just broke up with someone," Anders stated, "someone I cared for deeply. I still care for her, and the only thing I want is to get back together with her."

Jennifer's green eyes widened. Then, to Anders's dismay, they filled with tears. She lifted her hands to cover her face, her bracelets jingling. "Oh, I'm so embarrassed," she wailed. "I should've known better than to throw myself at you like this. I should've known you wouldn't want anything to do with me!"

"It's not that I—"

"I came all this way, and—and I really hoped you and I would click again," Jennifer finished. "I was really counting on that. I need a friend right now. After what happened with Bill, I . . . and now . . ."

She burst into a fresh spate of tears. Some people sitting at a nearby table turned to look at her. "Please stop crying, Jennifer," Anders begged, placing a hand on her arm. "Everything will be all right."

"No, it won't," she sobbed. "Not if you're going to send me straight back to Beverly Hills without giving me a chance to show you that we'd be good together, even better than before."

"I won't send you straight back to Beverly Hills," Anders began.

Jennifer smiled at him through her tears. "You mean, I can stay?"

"You said you were visiting your cousins, so I don't see why—"

"Oh, good." Anders's hand was still resting on her arm, and now she clasped it between both of her own. "You won't regret it, Anders. We'll have a great time. When is your senior prom, by the way?"

Anders raised his eyebrows, caught off guard by the question. "This Saturday night," he answered. "Why do you—"

"Fantastic!" Jennifer's tears had completely dried. "I'll still be in town. Isn't it, like, fate?"

Anders had heard through the grapevine that Susanna wasn't planning on going to the dance, and he didn't want to go either, if he couldn't go with her. "Jennifer, I really don't think—"

"But I had such a rotten time at my own prom." Jennifer's pretty face started to crumple again.

"Since you and your girlfriend broke up, can't you and I just go as friends?"

Anders sensed another onslaught of loud, hysterical tears just around the corner. "Jennifer, please," he said somewhat desperately. "I am not wishing to see you sad. But the prom——"

She sniffled. "I'm really sorry about what happened between us. Going to the prom would bring some closure, you know? It would make me so happy."

"Well . . ."

She took his hesitation for acquiescence. "It will be wonderful," she promised, beaming.

Anders smiled weakly. His head was spinning from the crazy, circuitous conversation. Had he just agreed to take Jennifer to the A.H.S. senior prom? *What have I gotten myself into?* he wondered.

"He's taking her to the prom!" Carly hissed.

It was Saturday morning, and the two girls were in downtown Altavista for haircuts and manicures. Susanna had wanted to cancel the beauty appointments, but Carly had insisted that they both needed a little pampering.

Now they sat in adjacent chairs inside Hannah's House of Style, their cuticles soaking in bowls of soapy, conditioned water, watching through the plate glass window as Jennifer Nelson emerged from a boutique across the street. There was no mistaking the purchase Jennifer had just made: She carried a long, puffy, plastic dress bag, the kind that might hold a prom gown.

Susanna looked away from the sight, her stomach lurching with misery. "Unbelievable," Carly declared with a toss of her head. "He's going to flaunt her in front of everybody. The nerve! I am so, *so* sorry, Suze."

"Me too," Susanna whispered.

"I almost wish I were going to the dance, just so I could torture those two with dirty looks."

Susanna managed a quivery smile. "You're a good friend, Carly."

"I wish she'd come in here so that I could tell her exactly what I think of her," Carly declared.

"Don't even say that!" Susanna couldn't imagine anything worse. But fortunately, Jennifer had disappeared.

Half an hour later, Susanna and Carly emerged from Hannah's House of Style with perfectly oval, pink-polished fingernails. "On to Heather's Hair Haven," Carly directed briskly.

Susanna trailed her friend glumly along the sidewalk. She had a hunch this was going to feel like the longest day of her life.

"You're sure you don't want to get together tonight?" Carly asked when she dropped Susanna off at her house just before lunchtime. "Go to a movie or something? It'll be so depressing sitting home alone."

"I just don't think I'd be very good company," Susanna apologized. "Anyhow, if you don't want to sit home alone, you don't have to. It's not too late to call Brad."

"I can't be seen at the senior prom with a sophomore," Carly declared, though without her usual conviction. Then she sighed. "Besides, I think it *is* too late. He got ticked off when he heard I was dating Colin. I guess it hurt."

"You really liked him, didn't you?"

"Yeah," Carly admitted. The two girls exchanged gloomy smiles. Then they hugged briefly. "Call me tomorrow?"

"Will do," Susanna promised.

The house was deserted. Her parents were sailing on the Bay with friends, and even Timber was absent, spending the day at the vet's to get a flea dip and teeth cleaning. Susanna drifted through the quiet rooms, trying to distract herself. She watched a little TV, read for a while, watered the garden, baked a batch of chocolate chip cookies. Nothing helped.

Finally, she flopped facedown on her bed. Carly had thought the beauty appointments would provide an emotional boost, but for Susanna, they'd had the opposite effect. *Talk about all dressed up and no place to go,* she thought mournfully.

Her closet door was ajar, and from her bed, she spotted a velvety glimmer of silvery blue. She'd never gotten around to returning the dress she'd bought in San Francisco when she thought she was going to the prom with Anders. At the sight of it, her eyes filled with bitter tears.

"I don't care that he's taking another girl to the prom and that *she* bought a dress at the Whitney Shop today," Susanna sobbed into her pillow. "I

161

don't care. I don't *care!*" But it simply wasn't true. She couldn't deny how much it hurt to think of Anders and Jennifer together.

I should have known better than to open up to him, Susanna thought. *I knew I'd only get hurt again.*

She rolled over on the bed, staring up at the ceiling. The afternoon sunlight bathed the room in a warm glow. In contrast, although her tears had dried, Susanna felt old, cold, and tired. She thought about the long months she'd struggled to recover from losing Seth, how much that process had taken out of her. She just didn't have the energy to deal with this new grief. And she recognized that it *was* genuine grief. She'd loved Anders as much as she'd loved Seth. And who knew how much more that love might have grown?

One thing was for sure, Susanna decided. In her experience, falling in love only led to pain. She was never, ever going to fall in love again.

FIFTEEN

"Y OU RESERVED A limousine, didn't you?"
Jennifer asked Anders. "And where are we
having dinner?"

It was Saturday afternoon, and Jennifer had driven
up to Altavista from her cousins' house in the city.
She'd tried on her new red dress for Anders, along
with high heels and jewelry, a complete sneak pre-
view. Now she was back in jeans and a snug-fitting
T-shirt, and they were sitting on the patio drinking
iced tea.

"I didn't make a reservation," Anders mumbled.

"We'll never get a table anywhere decent at the
last minute on prom night!" Jennifer chided. Then
she brightened again. "I know. We can pack a
picnic—bread, cheese, fruit, champagne—and have
the limo driver take us on a scenic tour through
Napa and Sonoma." Jennifer smiled. "Doesn't that
sound romantic?"

163

It did sound romantic. It also sounded like the last thing Anders felt like doing. Or maybe it was simply that Jennifer was the last person he felt like doing it with.

As Jennifer chattered on about how she planned to accessorize the red dress, Anders stared at her in mild disbelief. *I used to be in love with this girl!* he thought. He supposed he understood the attraction. He'd been drawn to Jennifer for the same reasons that many of the A.H.S. girls had been drawn to him initially: because she was a new face, foreign, exotic. But now that he saw her in her natural setting, Jennifer Nelson didn't seem so rare. In fact, she reminded him a lot of Tiffany, Chelsea, Rachel, and the others. She'd fit right in with that crowd.

"Jennifer, I think you should go home," Anders said suddenly.

She blinked her thick eyelashes. "Hmm? But I brought all the stuff I need for tonight over here." She ticked the items off on her fingers. "Dress, shoes, hose, jewelry, evening bag, makeup, hair spray, perfume." She smiled cheerfully. "I'm all set!"

Anders tried again. "What I'm meaning to say is that"—he waved vaguely in her direction—"this is not working out."

"I know you don't necessarily want us to get involved again," Jennifer reassured him, "and that's fine, although . . ." Leaning over, she brushed Anders's arm lightly with her fingertips. "Prom night *can* be magical. I think we should stay open to the possibilities."

Anders pulled his arm away from her touch. "No, Jennifer."

She sat back in her chaise longue, miffed. "Geez, Anders. Don't be so uptight."

"I am not uptight, but I still do not want to take you to the dance," he stated.

Jennifer folded her arms. "But I spent all that money on a new dress!"

"I'm sorry."

She stared at him for a long moment. When he didn't speak, she stood up, her posture rigid with indignation. *"Well."* She accidentally kicked over the lounge chair she'd just vacated, and it collapsed to the brick patio with a clatter. "I'm sure glad I traveled all the way to northern California to be treated like this."

"I'm sorry," Anders repeated sincerely. "I didn't mean to hurt your feelings."

Jennifer narrowed her green eyes. "Don't flatter yourself, Anders," she snapped as she flounced back into the house. "You're not *that* special."

He insisted on walking her to her car even though she refused to say another word to him. Dumping the dress bag and her other belongings unceremoniously into the backseat, Jennifer climbed behind the wheel of the Mustang convertible. She positioned her sunglasses firmly on the bridge of her small, straight nose, then tossed her hair one final, emphatic time. "Good-bye, Jennifer," Anders called as the Mustang roared off in a cloud of dust.

*   *   *

Susanna thought about calling Carly, then decided not to. She was the one, after all, who'd insisted that she didn't feel like going out. Carly had probably found something fun to do; she certainly wouldn't be sitting at home by the telephone.

Susanna put a kettle of water on the stove to boil, then leaned against the kitchen counter and gazed out the window. The sun was setting in a blaze of orange and scarlet that made the trees near her house look as if they were on fire. *At least I got outdoors this afternoon,* Susanna reflected. She'd gone for a long mountain bike ride, and the exercise had taken the edge off her dark mood. Now, after a hot shower and a light supper, she just felt weary.

The kettle whistled sharply. Susanna poured boiling water over a tea bag and watched it steep. She was about to remove the tea bag when the doorbell rang.

"Who could that be?" she wondered aloud, cinching the belt on her flannel bathrobe and running a hand through her still-damp hair. She wasn't exactly dressed for visitors. *Girl Scout cookies,* she thought. *Or a Little League fund-raiser, or someone selling newspaper subscriptions or collecting signatures for a petition.*

She padded into the front hall, the slate floor cool under her bare feet. "Who is it?" she called out.

There was no response. She peered through the narrow pane of glass next to the door, trying to get a look at the person who'd rung the bell. She didn't see anyone, but she did see a vehicle parked in the driveway. An unusual vehicle. A limousine!

Susanna gaped at the long, white car with its smoky, mysterious windows. Since when did the local Scout troop travel by limo? Confused, she opened the door.

A tall figure stepped forward from the shadows. For a split second, Susanna thought it must be the limousine driver—he was dressed in a black tuxedo with a white shirt and black bow tie. Then she recognized him. "Anders!" she gasped.

Anders had been holding one hand behind his back. Now he brought it forward, revealing a white box tied with a red ribbon. "Er, Susanna," he said, sounding nervous and formal. "I know this is the last minute. But if you do not have other plans this evening, I hope you will consider coming with me to the senior-class prom."

Susanna took the box. Inside was a wrist corsage of white roses and baby's breath, tied with a pale blue ribbon. She was nearly speechless with shock.

"Jennifer went back to Beverly Hills," Anders explained. "She came up here looking for something that I wasn't able to give her."

"You mean, you don't . . . you two aren't . . . ?"

"I don't care for Jennifer," Anders said quietly. "I care only for you, Susanna."

The sudden turn in events left Susanna breathless and weak-kneed. She didn't know whether to laugh or cry, so she continued to stand, mute as a statue, doing neither. *I feel like Cinderella,* she thought, dazed. *Hanging out in my bathrobe, and then all of a sudden, Prince Charming shows up in a limo!*

Anders cleared his throat again. "I know you do not want to be boyfriend and girlfriend," he said. "But perhaps . . . I hope . . . There is nothing on this earth that I would like more than for us to be friends again," he finished in a rush of heartfelt eloquence. "Will you go to the prom with me, as a friend?"

Anders had managed to put his feelings into plain, sweet words. Suddenly Susanna's own longings became crystal clear to her. She too knew exactly what she wanted. "I don't want to go to the prom as friends," she told Anders.

"Oh." His shoulders slumped. "I'm sorry. I should not have presumed—"

"No, wait." Before he could turn away, Susanna put a hand on his arm. She gazed up at him, her eyes glowing. "I *do* want to go with you, but not like that. I want to go to the prom as boyfriend and girlfriend."

His face lit up with joy. "Susanna," he said, his voice husky with emotion.

He reached for her, and she went to him eagerly, the corsage box dropping unnoticed to the ground between them. As Anders wrapped his arms around her, Susanna felt a sense of perfect happiness fill her, body and soul. She still wasn't sure precisely how she and Anders had found their way back to each other, but they were together again. And that, she thought as she lifted her face to his for a kiss, was all that really mattered.

★　　　★　　　★

"I bet the Altavista Country Club has never rocked like this!" Carly shouted to Susanna. A live band was jamming at the other end of the huge tent set up on the club's broad lawn. The airy space, lit only by tiny twinkling lights, was packed with wildly dancing bodies.

"I bet you're right!" Susanna shouted back.

It had taken the two best friends a good ten minutes to recover from the surprise of seeing each other at the prom after all. The stories had tumbled out in between hugs and laughter. "I'm so happy for you guys," Susanna said now to Carly and Brad.

Brad and Carly were standing with their arms wrapped around each other, and it looked as if they might never let go. "Me too," Carly said, radiant in her strapless black gown. She gazed at Brad with starry eyes.

"Me three," Brad said, an ear-to-ear grin on his face.

As Carly described it, just a few hours earlier she'd been sitting at home in sweatpants, eating Gummi Bears and channel surfing and feeling totally sorry for herself. Then she'd seen some ad on TV for some product that she couldn't remember, but there had been a guy and a girl in it getting romantic. At that moment, she'd realized that the only reason she was sitting home alone on prom night was because she was too proud to admit to herself and to the rest of Altavista High School that she was crazy about someone who was two grades behind her. So she'd called up Brad on the spot, and as luck would have it, he was home; the next thing they knew, they were at the prom together. Susanna was pretty sure that next to hers and Anders's, it was the most romantic tale she'd ever heard.

"There's one thing I don't get, Brad," said Susanna. "Where'd you find a tux at the last minute?"

"My dad's closet. You know those boring black-tie things doctors always have to go to. Dad's got a gut, though." Brad snapped his suspenders. "Thank goodness for these things!"

Still clinging to each other, Carly and Brad floated off in the direction of the band. Anders turned to Susanna. "So there is a happy ending for everyone, eh?" he noted, pulling Susanna close.

She curved her arms around his neck. "Looks like it," she agreed with a smile.

They shared a brief but meltingly sweet kiss. Just then, the band changed its beat, transitioning into a slow song. The intermingled crowd on the dance floor separated into couples, all holding each other tight.

"I can't believe we're actually here together," Susanna murmured as she and Anders swayed to the sultry rhythm.

"First, we planned to go to the dance as friends pretending to be more than friends," Anders recalled. "Then, we really *were* more than friends."

Susanna picked up the narrative. "Then we broke up, and we weren't going at all."

"I'm glad you changed your mind," he told her.

"So am I," she said, meaning it with all her heart. For a few minutes, they just held each other close. Susanna could feel Anders breathing, his heart beating in rhythm with her own. He was the first to speak. "I wish this night could last forever."

Susanna looked up at him, her eyes shining. "Me too. I wish we could always be together. But do you know what? I finally figured out that there's a difference between living for today and being afraid of tomorrow. You'll go back to Norway, but that doesn't have to mean we'll never see each other again."

"Yes," Anders said. "When the time comes, we will say *på gjensyn* instead of *farvel.*"

"What's the difference?" Susanna asked.

"*Farvel* means good-bye," Anders explained, "but *på gjensyn* is like the French *au revoir:* until we meet again."

"*På gjensyn.* I like that," she said.

"Anyway, you must come to Bergen," Anders told her. "It is a beautiful city. I want very much to show it to you. Come this summer! I will take you up north to see the midnight sun."

Susanna smiled. "Maybe I'd rather visit in the winter when it's dark all day."

Anders's arms tightened around her. "That has advantages too," he agreed. He kissed her softly on the lips. "I do promise you, though, that we will be together somehow."

Susanna nodded. She wasn't afraid of the future anymore, but nonetheless, she didn't want to think about it *too* much. Not when the present, this moment, being in Anders's arms, was so perfect.

They continued to dance. Susanna glimpsed

Carly and Brad, also in a blissful embrace. *What a night!* Susanna thought. *Our senior prom will be unforgettable after all.*

Susanna had never been quite so happy. There was only the slightest bittersweet edge to the frothy, delicious feeling that brimmed inside of her. Nothing could change the fact that Anders was leaving soon. But although their time together was measured, she wouldn't trade it for the world.

SIXTEEN

THERE WAS A senior–class graduation rehearsal scheduled for after school on Wednesday, but after the final bell, Susanna trotted out to the parking lot. She'd decided to run the risk of being a few minutes late for rehearsal. Another volunteer had taken over her art therapy program at the hospital—a wonderful senior citizen who'd actually once taught high-school art. Susanna knew Ms. McGarty would be wonderful, but she wanted to check in and make sure the transition was running smoothly. That, and she just plain missed the kids. If she'd learned one thing from losing Seth, it was how important it was to have a chance to say good–bye, to feel closure.

The first person she ran into in the pediatric cancer ward was Bob, the intern, who, as usual, looked as if he hadn't slept in a week. "Hear you're moving on to bigger and better things," he said. "Graduating."

"You too," Susanna noted.

"Yep. I've done my year here, and I'll finish up my residency at U.C.L.A.," Bob said. "But I'll miss this place, you know?"

"I'll miss it too," Susanna surprised herself by admitting.

"I've got to go do rounds." Bob folded her in a brotherly bear hug. "Good luck, kiddo. Hope I see you wearing one of these white coats someday."

She returned the hug, sudden tears stinging her eyes. "You never know."

She bypassed the nurses' station, saving those good-byes for later. At the patients' lounge, she stopped. The door was open a crack; she peeked through.

Ms. McGarty, an energetic, silver-haired woman in her late sixties, was in the center of a rapt group of children. "What do you think of that?" Mrs. McGarty wondered, holding up a reproduction of a pointillist painting. "Making a picture out of countless, tiny, different-colored dots?"

"Wacky!" a little boy exclaimed.

"Would you like to try it?" she asked.

There was a chorus of eager yeses. Susanna had been about to go into the room. Instead, she stepped back, carefully pulling the door closed. *Now that they have Ms. McGarty, they won't miss me,* she thought, feeling wistful. But that was okay. It was right. What mattered was that they have fun, that they get the chance to express the feelings that battled inside them: the fear, the anger, the hope. What mattered was that they keep up their spirits and work hard at getting better.

She walked back down the corridor toward the nurses' station, her chin high and her stride light. She felt good about the fact that she'd helped the kids for a while. She remembered her brief exchange with Bob. *"Hope I see you wearing one of these white coats someday. . . ."*

Susanna wasn't sure what she wanted for her future, but right now, she was comfortable with that. It meant that almost anything was possible. *Yep, you never know,* she thought.

"Look at Tiffany's yearbook picture," Carly whispered to Susanna, Kate, and Jin. "Is she wearing enough makeup or what?"

The Altavista High senior class had collected in the gymnasium for graduation rehearsal. Dressed in their rented caps and gowns, they were supposed to be organizing themselves alphabetically so that they could practice the procession, but no one was paying attention to Vice Principal McKenna's instructions. Yearbooks had been distributed during homeroom that morning, and the long-awaited volumes were being passed around, flipped through, laughed over, autographed.

"Check out the softball team picture," Jin said to Susanna, holding out her own book. "Don't we look great?"

Susanna adjusted her mortarboard, which was sliding down over her left ear, then examined

Tiffany's makeup *and* the softball team. "You're both right," she told Carly and Jin.

The vice principal was still shouting and waving her arms. "Okay, this time I mean it," she bellowed through a bullhorn. "Everybody's got a copy of the alphabetized class list. Find your place in line. If you can't manage this, none of you graduate. It's that simple!"

Susanna and her friends went their separate ways. Still chattering and laughing, the seniors milled about the gym in what appeared to be total chaos. But miraculously, Susanna found her spot between Claire Rafferty and Leo Reynolds. In five minutes flat, the whole class was lined up.

Ms. McKenna read through the list. There was some minor reshuffling. When everyone was ready, the tape-recorded strains of "Pomp and Circumstance" began echoing through the gym.

Even though it was just a rehearsal, Susanna felt her heart beat faster. In less than a week, she'd be a high-school graduate! Over summer vacation, she'd register for her fall courses at Stanford. She'd find out who her freshman roommates were going to be. Next thing she knew, it would be September and she'd be moving into a dorm on campus. Her college years would begin.

The students marched around the gym, then filed into rows of folding chairs. Susanna sat down, her yearbook on her lap. As Ms. McKenna explained the order of the ceremony—speeches, choral music, presentation of diplomas, more speeches, recessional—Susanna opened the yearbook and started turning the pages.

She passed quickly over the sections devoted to underclassmen, faculty, athletics, clubs. At the beginning of the senior-class pictures, she stopped.

It was the first time she'd gotten up the nerve to look at Seth's memorial page, although people had been coming up all day to hug her, share a few tears, and say how great it was. Now Susanna gazed down at the collage of black-and-white photographs and the brief, handwritten remembrances of his closest buddies.

Seth smiled up at her from the picture in the middle of the page, the one she'd contributed, the one at Half Dome. Susanna touched his face lightly with her fingertip. *It's so strange,* she thought, the old familiar ache filling her heart. They were all in the book, every single A.H.S. senior. A moment in their lives was frozen there, preserved forever. But for Seth, that moment was the end. As the rest of them marched on, he'd remain behind, always seventeen.

Susanna swallowed the salty tears stinging her throat. Her finger trailed down the page, tracing the words at the bottom, words scripted in her own handwriting. *"We'll miss you, Seth. We'll never forget you."*

She flipped through the portraits of the rest of her classmates without really seeing them. Then she came to the last section in the yearbook: pictures from the senior prom, hastily put together right before the yearbook went to the printer. There was one of her and Anders with Carly and Brad, raising their punch cups in a celebratory toast.

Susanna gazed at the picture for a long moment. Then she closed the book and folded her hands on top of it.

Ms. McKenna was still talking. "When the last name is read, you can do what seniors usually do—throw your caps in the air, what have you."

"Pop champagne corks!" a voice shouted.

The vice principal smiled. "As I said. Then you'll march out of the gym in an orderly fashion. Note my emphasis on 'orderly.' After that, you're free."

"And it's party time!" someone else called out.

Susanna laughed along with everyone else. *Free,* she reflected. Yes, that was exactly right. She was free, as free as a bird. Free to travel wherever she wanted to go, to learn whatever she wanted to learn, to become whoever she wanted to be. *I'm so lucky. We're all so lucky,* she thought. She made a silent promise to herself . . . and to Seth: *Life is such a precious gift. I'll always make the most of it.*

Anders bicycled up to the Collinas' house the afternoon before A.H.S. graduation. He wouldn't be participating in the ceremony—he'd receive his own diploma from his Bergen high school later that summer—but of course he'd watch from the audience. He'd just gone into town to pick up the graduation present he'd ordered for Susanna: a silver locket engraved on the back with the words "I love you, Susanna—Anders." No date; he wanted the sentiment to be timeless.

At the foot of the driveway, Anders applied the

brakes. Leaning the bike against the fence, he checked the mailbox. Pulling out the stack of mail, he tucked it under his arm, then walked the bike the rest of the way.

He didn't notice the thick letter from Stanford until he was walking into the house. When he saw the return address, he halted in the entryway, his heart hammering inside his chest. *It couldn't be,* he thought.

His fingers shook a little as he tore open the envelope. A whole sheaf of paper slid out. As he read the top page, a smile spread slowly across his face.

He'd pretty much given up hope, but the impossible had happened. *"Ja,"* he exclaimed, thrusting a triumphant fist into the air. "I'm in!"

Anders strode down the hall to the kitchen. Picking up the phone, he began to dial his parents' number in Bergen. He had to tell them immediately about this new development, that he'd be flying home to Norway in two days as planned, but returning to the States in the fall.

Before he'd finished dialing the international number, though, Anders hung up the phone in order to dial a different number—just seven digits, a local call. There was someone else who should be the first to hear his news.

"Hei, Susanna?" he said when she answered the telephone. "Let's go for a walk on the beach. I'll be right over to pick you up."

Susanna was going over her graduation party checklist with her mother when Anders called. "I think we've got everything under control, Mom," she concluded cheerfully. "Food, drinks, cups, plates, napkins, balloons, streamers. All we need to buy at the last minute is ice."

"Your dad and I will help you set up tomorrow afternoon, and then we'll clear out of your way," Dr. Reyes promised.

Roberto Reyes strode into the kitchen at that moment, carrying a small cardboard box. "Hey, you mean I'm not invited to the party of the decade?" he asked.

Susanna laughed. "Sure, you're invited, Dad. For the first five or ten minutes."

He shook his head, pretending to glower. "We old people never have any fun."

Dr. Reyes gave her husband a hug around the waist. "We've got theater tickets," she reminded him. "That's not so bad."

"Listen, I've got to run," Susanna told her parents. She stuck the shopping list back on the fridge with a magnet. "Anders'll be here in a minute."

"Speaking of which . . ." Mr. Reyes held out the box he'd been holding. "Just a little graduation something for the two of you," he explained.

Susanna opened the box. Inside, two picture frames nestled in a bed of tissue paper. Her father had painted the hand-carved wood in different soft colors, picking up hues from the photograph he'd placed in each one: Anders and Susanna on prom night.

"Oh, Dad, they're beautiful," Susanna declared, her eyes misty. "That was so thoughtful of you."

Her father dropped a kiss on her cheek. "I love you, kiddo."

"Love you too, Dad."

She took one of the frames right to her bedroom to display on her nightstand. She was tucking the other into her backpack when Anders drove up.

Half an hour later, they were walking hand in hand along a sandy Pacific beach, the cold surf splashing their bare feet. "You sounded kind of funny on the phone before," Susanna told Anders, swinging his hand. "Is anything wrong?"

He shook his head. "I just wanted to see you," he said. "Tomorrow will be so busy, and then on Sunday . . ."

He didn't need to finish the sentence. They both knew what was happening on Sunday: Anders would board a plane at San Francisco International Airport for the first leg of his trip back to Norway.

Susanna squeezed his hand tightly, unable to speak. She didn't trust her self-control; she was already on the verge of bawling at the thought that this was probably her last walk along the beach with Anders. For a long, long time anyway.

"Susanna," Anders said. He stopped at the water's edge, taking both her hands. She faced him, her eyelashes damp with tears. "I have something for you."

"I have something for you too," she said, thinking of the picture frame.

"Me first." Releasing her hands, Anders took a small jewelry box from the pocket of his khaki shorts. "I hope you like it," he said somewhat shyly.

Susanna opened the box. When she read the engraving on the silver locket, the tears spilled from her eyes. "Oh, Anders."

"That's not all," he said quickly. "I have another present for you."

"You do?"

This time, he took a piece of paper from his pocket. Without an explanation, he handed it to Susanna.

She unfolded it, still sniffling. "'Dear Mr. Lund,'" she read out loud. "'We are pleased to inform you that because you were very high on our waiting list, we are now able to offer you a place in the freshman class—'" Susanna stopped, blinking in astonishment as her fingers touched the Stanford letterhead. Then she looked up at Anders, her eyes wide. "Anders, does this mean . . . ?"

"Yes." He grinned. "I'm going to Stanford!"

As it sank in, a smile covered Susanna's face. "You're going to Stanford," she echoed. "With me!"

"With you," he confirmed. Suddenly, he looked serious. "I hope it's okay, Susanna. I didn't tell you about this before because I didn't think I would get in. Maybe you had gotten used to the idea that I would go away, and now I am going to be around after all. . . ."

Susanna gazed up at Anders. Tears filled her eyes once more. Not that long ago, she'd dreamed of making plans like this with Seth. Then Seth died, and all the hopes of her heart were crushed. *I've come so far,* she thought, amazed by the unexpected, wonderful path her life had taken. She'd be going to college with her boyfriend after all . . . her boyfriend Anders Lund. And the important thing was, she didn't feel guilty. She didn't feel as if she were being disloyal to Seth, the boy she'd once loved and would never forget. She was looking forward again instead of back into the past, and that was the way it should be.

"Of course I want you around!" Susanna said, throwing her arms around Anders.

Their lips met in a long, sweet kiss that was like a pledge—a pledge that they'd always be there for each other. "I would've been okay if you went back to Norway, you know," Susanna told Anders.

"I know," he said. "You're strong."

She smiled broadly. "But this is going to be so much better!"

Anders picked her up, swinging her in a joyful circle. Laughing, Susanna felt the moment enter her body and spirit. It was a moment bursting with the warmth of sunshine, love, expectation, and hope. All the very best things in the world.

Anders placed her back down on the sand, but his arms remained clasped firmly around her. The clear blue sky arched over them, the ocean surf rolled in at their feet, and the future stretched out before them, filled with limitless promise. As they kissed again, Susanna knew she'd always remember this place, this time, this feeling. *It's our happy ending,* she thought. *It's our new beginning.*

Do you ever wonder about falling in love? About members of the opposite sex? Do you need a little friendly advice but have no one to turn to? Well, that's where we come in . . . Jenny and Jake. Send us those questions you're dying to ask, and we'll give you the straight scoop on life and love in the nineties.

DEAR JAKE

Q: *My boyfriend, Ian, and I have been together for over a year. Recently, his cousins came to town for a visit, and it was all Ian could talk about for weeks before. I couldn't wait to meet these guys that he was so excited to see. But his cousins were here for three days, and he never invited me over to meet them. One night, he even called me and told me he'd be late for our date because he was hanging out with them. I was fine with it, but I don't understand why we couldn't all hang out together. What should I do?*

SC, San Diego, CA

A: This is definitely something you should feel free to talk to Ian about. If you two have been together for so long, there's no reason he should feel weird about you meeting his cousins. He probably just didn't realize you were so interested. Just sit him down and tell him he hurt your feelings when he didn't ask if you wanted to hang out with them. He'll probably either tell you that he never thought of it because he was so busy, or that he didn't think you'd want to hang out with a bunch of guys. Either way, he'll realize it was wrong of him not to include you, and he'll make sure to ask the next time. But the next time a situation like this comes up, make sure you express interest beforehand. That way, he'll know for sure that you want to be included, and no one will get hurt.

Q: *I recently started going out with this guy who has always had a reputation for being a player. He's gone out with a couple of my friends in the past but never very seriously. With me, he says it's different. He told me he's never felt this way before and he feels like he's falling in love. I have so much fun with him and he always makes me laugh, but I don't know if I should believe him. What if he's just feeding me a line?*

PF, Danbury, CT

A: Some people will tell you guys never change . . . but luckily (or maybe unluckily), I'm not one of those people. No matter how many girls a guy has dated in the past, sooner or later he's bound to find one who makes him want to stick around. For some guys, this happens while they're still in high school; for others, it may not happen until they're in retirement. At any rate, it's entirely possible that he's telling the truth, and why not? A great person like you shouldn't be surprised to win a guy's heart. What you should do is find out if he used the same line on any of your friends. If he did, you can't believe him. But if this is truly a new feeling for him, I'm sure it took a lot of guts for him to express it, and you shouldn't take that lightly.

DEAR JENNY

Q: *Every time I like a guy, I turn into a complete idiot. I just made it into all-state choir, and at the first practice, I met this incredibly cute boy named Ross. Right after we said hello, I tripped over a riser and caused a domino effect, making people fall all over one another. Later, I tried out for a solo I knew I could do, but I saw him smiling at me and proceeded to go horribly off-key. By the end of the day, I was too embarrassed to go near him, so I bolted for the door before he could say anything. I know he thinks I'm a loser now. What can I do?*

SR, Wilmington, DE

A: Chances are this guy doesn't think you're a loser. Anyone can trip, and I'm sure Ross knows anyone can go off-key. But if you think you have a problem with nervousness around guys, there is something you can do about it. You have to realize that Ross isn't standing there waiting for you to do something stupid. In fact, he's probably wondering if he has something stuck between his teeth, or thinking about his next solo and whether or not *he'll* mess up. Often, we think everyone around us is noticing every little thing we do, but in reality, they're wrapped up in their own lives. Once you realize that no one is watching and waiting for you to trip up, you'll become more comfortable with yourself. And everyone else, including Ross, will notice your new confidence too.

Q: *My boyfriend, Rick, is trying to make me feel guilty because I've missed his last two soccer games. But he's never come to one of my tennis matches. He always says he has to practice or he already has plans. How can I make him understand how much this hurts?*

KF, Cranston, RI

A: Be honest with him. Tell him you really enjoy his soccer games, but you can't attend every single one. Then tell him that it hurts your feelings that he can't find time to do the things that are important to you. Tell him you don't expect him to be there all the time, but he could at least come to a home match. If he says he has plans, point out that the schedule is set at the beginning of the season, just like his soccer schedule, and he should be able to work around that. Hopefully, he's reasonable enough to see that a relationship requires give-and-take; otherwise it's not a relationship.

Do you have questions about love? Write to:

Jenny Burgess or Jake Korman
c/o Daniel Weiss Associates
33 West 17th Street
New York, NY 10011